Purapurawhetū

Purapurawhetū

BRIAR GRACE-SMITH

HUIA PUBLISHERS

First published in 1999 by Huia Publishers,
39 Pipitea Street, P O Box 17-335,
Wellington, Aotearoa New Zealand.

ISBN 0-908975-78-3

Text © Briar Grace-Smith
This edition © Huia Publishers
The oriori on page 46 and the haka on page 104
were composed by Kohai Grace.

All applications to:
Playmarket
PO Box 9767
Wellington, New Zealand
ph 64-4-382 8462

Ka tohia tēnei pakiwaitara ki a Kohai rāua ko Joanne. He tino ātaahua ngā tukutuku a ngā tokorua nei.

Acknowledgements

This play was rewritten for publication while the writer was the 1998 Writer in Residence at Massey University. Its first performance was supported by a grant from Creative New Zealand.

I would like to acknowledge Huia Publishers for continuing to promote the writing and development of our Māori writers. A special thanks to Playmarket, Jean Betts, Mere Boynton and Taki Rua Productions for their support.

To Cathy Downes for your encouragment and belief in this work and to the original cast, musican, lighting, set and creative designers for their great generosity and skill. To Kerehi Waiariki Dick Grace for the Māori translations and to Kohai Grace for composing waiata.

Finally to my partner Himiona and our tamariki for your advice and patience.

Ngā mihi aroha ki a koutou!

Contents

Introduction

Purapurawhetū is set in a small coastal town, Te Kupenga. The name Te Kupenga – The Net – seems to speak of a historically nurturing relationship between a fishing people and the sea. However, the bonds between people and place are not always formed in the positive: they assert themselves through things as minor as the inconvenience of duty, as major as imprisonment of the mind or the body. As *Purapurawhetū* is played out it becomes apparent that the place name Te Kupenga is cast in the negative and directly comments on the characters' situation. The net has drawn the characters back home, caught them in the overlapping and knotted edges of sea, land and the night sky. Interlacing the depressed present and the vibrant past, the play aches for Te Kupenga's renewal, when the strands of the net may cease to oppress and limit, but bind and strengthen.

The chance to rejuvenate an economically and spiritually depressed town hinges on the successful utterance of an ōhākī, a dying speech. A formal parallel to this ōhākī is provided by the gradual weaving of diverse strands into a tukutuku panel, which provides an overarching Māori pattern for the play. As the ōhākī is uttered, the tukutuku panel is woven, and as the panel is woven, so the diverse strands of the play are gathered together from different artistic domains, places, languages, popular cultures, and local and national politics.

Purapurawhetū opens during the post-MMP political period of the 1996–1998 coalition between National and New Zealand First. Winston Peters is deputy prime minister, Tau Henare minister of Māori affairs, and their party, New Zealand First, presents itself as the obvious vehicle for an ambitious Māori male entering his middle years who would like to gain parliamentary political power. Against this national situation, *Purapurawhetū* has a concern with the nature of rangatiratanga and the way that mana is exercised through local development, for success on a local level will presumably assist a bid for success on a national level. In the figures of Mata and Tyler, the play contrasts different motivations and leadership styles, addressing power within the hapū, as well as looking cynically at leadership on a national level.

As a countercheck to this potential for local and national power, *Purapurawhetū* is also formed by the characters' shared experience of physical and cultural loss, which takes many forms. Hohepa's great loss and ensuing search overarches others' less-prominent searching. For example, after the loss of Kui's family's ancestral land, she was sold to a gumdigger. She fled her life as a slave in the gumfields of Muriwhenua and became transient. Unable to return home, she ended up in Te Kupenga in the 1950s. In her disinheritance she is a dramatized version of many people, for gumdigging had serious effects on the iwi of Muriwhenua. The Waitangi Tribunal's *Muriwhenua Land Report* provides a broad historical overview of the effects of gumdigging:

> Maori economic survival, from after the Government purchases to the present, can be traced through two overlapping stages, gumdigging and land development. The story of Maori gumdigging in the north is one of abject poverty from which the people did not begin to recover until recently. The second stage, land development, describes a struggle to rebuild a people on poor and marginal territory. [1]

At the Tribunal hearing, there was debate between claimants and the Crown over whether the gumdigging was carried out of necessity, or if it was carried out voluntarily, with its rewards proving more seductive than those offered by more traditional activities such as crop planting. However,

> [t]he effects on Maori health and education were devastating. With long periods of camping in the gumfields without proper sanitation and unhealthy living areas in swamps, high rates of death and disease became apparent, particularly among the children. In the early decades of the twentieth century, with falling gum prices and loss of control of their lands, local people were locked even more tightly into poverty and deprivation with little opportunity for any economic development. [2]

Closely associated with the economic changes underpinning the play are the losses and gains (perhaps 'substitutions' is a more appropriate term) of cultural change. A major loss is signified by namelessness. The events of the play are bracketed between namelessness and naming, formlessness and substance, beginning in the early morning with the voice of Bubba declaring his insubstantiality, ending with the voice of the newly-named Awatea celebrating whanaungatanga. Grace-Smith never explicitly provides an English translation of the name Awatea, and so posits the naming and the new beginning as occurring in Māori terms.

Tyler's dispossession, or formless beginning, is a generation or two further on from Kui's. To Ramari, Mata says that 'Tyler's people are the nameless, faceless, invisible dwellers of the street ....' Completely urbanized, his origins are lost, and popular culture provides a substitute, itself becoming a point of origin. The story of Tyler's naming is playful and subversive, deftly documenting the Americanization of Māori culture. Tyler tells Ramari that he is named after the 'great American tipuna Mere Tyler Moa'. By the parodic use of transliteration, he declares his virtual whakapapa. Stretching back to an unnamed movie from Mary Tyler Moore's long career (perhaps *X-15* (1961), *Change of Habit* (1970), in which Mary Tyler Moore played a nun to Elvis Presley's Dr

John Carpenter, or *Ordinary People* (1980)), Tyler's lineage
signals the danger of (cultural) extinction – Moore to Moa.
This danger is not lost on Tyler: 'Doris and the rest of them,
they treat me like whānau. But sometimes I think about it,
the truth, and I freak right out.'

While the identity issues involved in journeying from the
papakāinga to live in the city are a prominent feature of
contemporary Māori writing, the return home to the
papakāinga and the revitalization of Māori institutions has
less frequently received substantial treatment. Coming back
home is the subject of Patricia Grace's *Potiki*, and this return
signals the beginning of a serious cultural revival, which
Roimata sees as the chance to tell 'our own-centre stories....'[3]
It is an internally unproblematic return, for the novel's crisis
comes from outside the hapū. By contrast, while
Purapurawhetū similarly begins to explore relocation
following dislocation, the play problematizes the return home
itself by looking inwards. The way that it does this looking
is to use language as a sign of origination, wandering and
returning.

Language is a potent sign of the scattered places characters
have been to before they are gathered in by Te Kupenga. A
rapid shifting between languages and styles evokes the
characters' backgrounds. This shifting is known to linguists
as code switching (between languages) and style shifting
(between styles within a language).[4] The characters' code
switching, from English to Māori and back again, is
accompanied by rapid changes of language style, sometimes
skidding through mud, sometimes getting aerial.

Code switching has different effects depending on whether
the play is read or seen in performance, and, of course,
depending on the reader or audience member's command of

the Māori language and of Māori English.

The easiest switch for the non-reader of Māori to accommodate is where there is an imbalance in comprehension between characters, so an explanation to one character becomes a translation for some readers or audience members, as when Tyler explains to Ramari that an ōhākī is 'like a legacy ....' At times, the use of Māori language cuts straight to deep concerns. The reverse also holds, where earnestness can presage deflation.

In this text, single words have not been glossed, but phrases and sentences have been translated and footnoted, as there lies the most room for meaning to be misconstrued. For viewers of the play, there is a boundary-maintaining use of language, limiting access to meaning only to those more fluent in the Māori language. The footnoted translations used in the text set the doors of meaning ajar, but they do not fully open them. The play in performance can exclude an audience member from complete involvement. This opens up potential in performance to involve the audience in dramatized cross-cultural situations.

This new orthodoxy, which occurs also in Samoan theatre, differs considerably from the treatment of the Māori language in Hone Tuwhare's *In the Wilderness Without a Hat*, which premiered in 1985. The set instructions specify how the Māori language is to be treated: 'A P.A. system ... will also carry the voices (male and female) of "Interpreters," who must cue in precisely at the end of spoken words in Maori. Their voices must be flat, discreet, confidential.'[5]

Tension and contrast between characters is accentuated by constant switching of register, or style. To Hohepa's whakataukī-influenced lofty discourse, Aggie replies with low burlesque:

> HOHEPA: ... Like Kōpū, the morning star, your beauty has me spellbound. I ... I think I would like to weave it into a blanket, so whenever I felt the sunset too diluted, or the sea too grey, I could wrap myself up and let the very richness of you sink into my pores.

> AGGIE: Well. That's what happens when you're around too many people with the same smile. You long for a bit of pepper on your chops.

Hohepa's declaration of romantic love uses the mythic comparison between Kōpū and the beauty of a woman: 'Me te mea ko Kōpū ka rere i te pae' (Like Venus as it rises above the horizon). Aggie, however, sees it as adding a hot and pungent flavour to the same old carnality.

Cultural importation adds spice to the fecund mix of languages and styles. When young Hohepa and Aggie court, they dance the rumba, a dance of Cuban origin. Aggie's discourse has much in common with the type of movie that gives so much life to Witi Ihimaera's novel *Bulibasha*: Aggie speaks of 'cowboys' at a dance hall called the 'Half-Moon Corral'.

Redmer Yska writes of country and western singer Johnny Cooper whose stage name, the 'Maori Cowboy', revealed the country influence of Gene Autry, the 'Singing Cowboy'. HMV, the record company, asked Cooper to record a pre-emptive cover of Bill Haley and the Comets' 'Rock around the Clock' before it was released in New Zealand. The record was unsuccessful. '... I didn't feel it; I was a country singer', said Cooper. Yska writes:

> Cooper's discomfort with the alien style was increased when HMV insisted that jazzmen Ken Avery and his Rockin' Rhythm

play the backing, rather than his usual band, the Range Riders. The resulting song was an embarrassment and HMV's attempt to cash in on what *Truth's* Middlebrow column described as the 'new rock'n'roll craze' flopped.[6]

In this conflation of musical genres – rock, jazz, country – can be seen something of the way that the flirtation between the South Pacific and the United States occurs: in part economically overdetermined, in part voluntarily imported, in part occurring by substituting one genre for another. Reflecting the continuing process of drawing on the musical and linguistic resources of the United States, the play's language moves between young Hohepa and Aggie's musical and filmic intertexts to Tyler's hip-hop slang: 'But you the man eh Koro? One day you're gonna snap right out of it and give Te Kupenga a real shake up. Yeah. Fuck yeah, you da man.'

The various codes and styles woven accretively into the texture of the play provide a cumulative richness. Reviewers of the 1997 Taki Rua production hinted at this effect:

> So densely is this play written that the first part requires steady concentration, which is ultimately rewarded when its slow-burning narrative explodes into an extraordinarily exciting and moving climax.[7]

The play's accumulating strands are woven into a Māori design. A design element can evoke a wider world. In this regard, *Purapurawhetū* has some parallels with Hirini Melbourne's prescriptive model for literature written in Māori:

> The Māori writer who wishes to begin writing in Māori needs some concrete means of drawing on the general heritage of Māori culture in order to express the way of seeing the world that is

particular to Māori people. One way of conceiving how this might be accomplished is to adopt the symbol of the whare whakairo. The whare whakairo is a symbol of cultural unity, a place of shelter and peace. It is a place where knowledge is stored and transmitted and where the links with one's past are made tangible. The whare whakairo is a complex image of the essential continuity between the past and the present that indicates how contemporary writing in the Māori language might express the world of the Māori people.[8]

Describing a possible way in which the composition of the whare whakairo could assist the Maori writer Melbourne discusses the building's aspects, finishing with 'the decorative art works of kōwhaiwhai, whakairo, and tukutuku [which] represent the various formal devices at the disposal of composers, poets and/or orators to clothe their ideas in seductive and elaborate styles and flourishes.'[9]

In *Purapurawhetū*, the art of raranga is a way of thinking about rangatiratanga, art, values and traditions when they are met by extraordinary events. The pattern of the tukutuku panel orders the play by paralleling the ōhākī, by visually representing to future generations the oral revelation of painful events that occurred some time ago, and by signifying the rightful order of things. As a technical device in Māori writing it finds parallels in novels by Māori writers. Keri Hulme's *The Bone People* uses the spiral motif as a way of structuring time and controlling the open-ended and growing implications of the narrative, while Witi Ihimaera's *The Matriarch* includes a poutama tukutuku pattern which symbolizes the education of the novel's protagonist.

Related to this, the work of the poet, composer, storyteller (and playwright) is sometimes self-assayed through internal comparison with other more traditional artistic domains.

Hone Tuwhare's poem 'On a Theme by Hone Taiapa' likens the poet to a carver, for example, while elsewhere the idea of weaving, pervasive in indigenous writing, is used as a metaphor for cultural continuance. Trixie Te Arama Menzies' poem 'Harakeke' views harakeke as: ' ... homely, strong as a woman built for childbearing/ Provider of warp and weft, the fabric of being.'[10]

Tyler, in conversation with Ramari, explicitly compares Kui as storyteller to a weaver, saying she is an 'awesome weaver', who 'doesn't even need to use her hands.' This comparison is also brought about in performance by juxtaposing weaving with storytelling.

> KUI (*looking down at the bundle in her arms*): ... One hot day, while Hohepa was out chasing cows and Aggie was busy sewing on her new shiny black Singer, Mata took Bubba down to the beach. (*She weaves Purapurawhetū.*) Stole his father's fishing boat and put wee Bubba inside. He rowed, he rowed as far as his puffy 12 year-old arms could take him. Then he stopped, put down the oars. (*She stops work.*) Did he look into your eyes then, Bubba? ...

The panel embodies stories passed down to the following generations, and it cannot be woven until the story is known. As the panel is finished, the story of its local meaning is told to the new generation, and succession can occur. Ramari, however, does not finish the panel. She ties two stitches upside down for her 'scabby mokos' to see in fifty years time. This hints that the story is not 'tied off', that it has not ended, that closure is provisional. The story will be retold time and again, never complete.

An early version of *Purapurawhetū* was first published as a short story entitled 'Puku Up, Puku Down',[11] which differed substantially in the interpretation given to the tukutuku panel. In the short story, the panel embodies an iwi. The narrator's Aunty Esther explains:

> It talks about the people of your iwi. There are the carvers, and the weavers, like you. Then there's the kaipakanga, the fighters – they are the movers and the shakers. The kaimahi, these people are the doers, they are the cooks and the workers and without them we would accomplish nothing. And finally we have the kaikorero, the orators and storytellers. I am one of those. (49)

Purapurawhetū works on a different scale to the short story. The intertextual relationship between the play and older texts is quite loose by comparison with Potiki, which closely uses the narratives of Christ and Māui in the character of Tokowaru-i-te-Marama, or *The Matriarch*, where the narrator takes his name from Tamatea, captain of the *Takitimu* waka. His rivalry with Toroa (named after the captain of the *Mataatua* waka) is the basis of a significant sub-plot.

Purapurawhetū is connected to intertexts elsewhere. It evokes associations with classical literature through Tyler's weaving. In the opening scene, Tyler's frustration suggests that there is something beyond his control holding him back from completing the panel. This suspended completion finds a correspondent intertext in Homer's *Odyssey*. By deferring the completion of a piece of weaving – Odysseus's burial shroud – Penelope postpones her availability for marriage. Tyler's dilatory tukutuku panel weaving is a similarly strategic means of deferral. He declares that, 'You fullas can just sit here chewing your nails till I've finished this panel, and if I'm still weaving on the day the marae opens, tough. I'll be on permanent exhibition.' If the stories that are to give the panel its local significance within the whare at Te Kupenga are not known, the panel cannot be completed. On a deep level, Tyler is aware that it isn't possible to complete a spiritual piece of work when there is metaphysical resistance of the order of that offered by the lost and insubstantial Bubba.

Purapurawhetū, in its gatherings from past and present, points to the on-going working and re-working of culture, the warp and weft of which is always being woven. It hopes to shape the accidental and clumsy chaos of 'poking out knots' and 'puku the wrong-way-ups' through knowing and aware artifice. By looking inwards to people caught in its net the play asks a people who are heir to intergenerational trauma and displacement to become agents of their own healing, for, to Hohepa, there are deep interconnections: 'None of us are blameless'. *Purapurawhetū* is at once a gathering of the lost in an orienting pattern, an inexorable story, and a quiet and deep searching, in the same place, through the years, for a lost treasure.

John Huria

Editor

Notes

1 Waitangi Tribunal, *Muriwhenua Land Report* (Wai 45), Wellington, GP Publications, 1997, p. 355

2 Ibid, 365-6

3 Patricia Grace, *Potiki*, Penguin: Auckland, 1986, p. 39.

4 See Elizabeth Gordon and Mark Williams, 'Raids on the Articulate: Code-Switching, Style-Shifting and Post-Colonial Writing', *Journal of Commonwealth Literature*, (33:2), 1998, pp. 75–96 for a discussion of issues raised by code switching. See also Roger Robinson, ' "The

Strands of Life and Self": The Oral Prose of Patricia Grace', *CRNLE Reviews Journal*, (1), 1993, pp. 13–27.

5   Hone Tuwhare, 'In the Wilderness Without a Hat', in *He Reo Hou: 5 Plays by Maori Playwrights*, Wellington: Playmarket, 1991, p. 59.

6   Redmer Yska, *All Shook Up: The Flash Bodgie and the Rise of the New Zealand Teenager in the Fifties*, Auckland: Penguin, 1993, p. 140.

7   Susan Budd, 'Production with Humanity and Hope', *The Dominion* 23 May 1997. See also Denis Welch, 'A New Classic', *NZ Listener*, 14 June 1997.

8   Melbourne, Hirini. 1991. 'Whare Whakairo: Maori "Literary" Traditions', in: *Dirty Silence: Aspects of Language and Literature in New Zealand,* Graham McGregor and Mark Williams, eds., p. 133.

9   Ibid, 134.

10 Trixie Te Arama Menzies, *Uenuku*, Auckland: Waiata Koa, 1986.

11 Briar Smith, 'Puku Up, Puku Down', *Huia Short Stories 1995*, Huia Publishers: Wellington, 1995, 45–50.

Preface

While helping with tukutuku panels in preparation for the opening of Te Heke Mai Raro at Hongoeka Marae, I began to think about the stories behind traditional carving and weaving patterns such as Purapurawhetū. Many hold within them the rich language and epic themes of love, jealousy and revenge. I became inspired then to write a play where as the tukutuku panel Purapurawhetū is being woven, its story unfolds around the weaver. While writing about the tragedy that takes place within *Purapurawhetū* it became clear that this must also be a story of forgiveness and healing. In order to move into the future we must make peace with our past.

Ko ngā tātai whetū ki te rangi, mau tonu, mau tonu.
Ko ngā tātai tangata ki te whenua, ngaro noa, ngaro noa.

Briar Grace-Smith

First Performance

Purapurawhetū was the first Taki Rua production to be performed at Downstage Theatre. It premiered in May 1997 with the following cast and production team:

MATAWERA	Jim Moriarty
KUI/AGGIE ROSE	Vanessa Rare
KORO HOHEPA	Hemi Rurawhe
RAMARI	Kirsty Hamilton
TYLER	Bradley Carroll
Director	Cathy Downes
Sound Designer/Composer	Himiona Grace
Set Designers	Diane Prince and Mark McEntyre
Lighting Designer	Helen Todd
Costume Designer	Deborah Ruffell

The oriori (lullaby) and Awatea's chant were composed by Kohai Grace.

Awatea's chant was performed by Alair Smith.

The voice of Awatea – Himiona Grace (junior)

Set

There were two spaces in Purapurawhetū. One was the whare raranga where Tyler worked, the focal point being a large tukutuku panel. The panel was symbolised by a framework made from kōrari, the stalks of the flax flower. The other space was the beach, where Hohepa spent most of his time searching in the water amongst the rocks.

The Whānau

KUI/AGGIE ROSE:
In her sixties. Aggie Rose and Kui are the same person and are played by the same actor. Kui's eyesight is bad and she is arthritic. She uses a stick to help her walk, a veil covers her face. Aggie Rose is the 'memory' of Kui as she was in her youth, tough and vivacious.

KORO HOHEPA:
In his sixties. Hohepa was once married to Aggie Rose. Matawera's father.

MATAWERA:
In his forties. Has recently moved back to Te Kupenga.

TYLER:
In his early twenties. Weaver. He is a whāngai (adopted child) and has lived in Te Kupenga since he was three.

RAMARI:
In her late teens. She has recently moved to Te Kupenga from Christchurch.

AWATEA or BUBBA:
Awatea is the spirit of the baby who Hohepa and Aggie Rose had together. He is never seen and is heard as a whisper. His voice is recorded.

Location

Purapurawhetū is set in the 1990s in the depressed seaside community of Te Kupenga. The iwi are now working to establish a new wharenui in the hope that it will regenerate life and bring home the scattered whānau.

The memory scenes are set in the 1950s, when Hohepa, Aggie Rose and the village of Te Kupenga were in their prime.

Act One

Scene One

Puku Up

It is early morning. The stage is lit in cool blues and greens. HOHEPA stares out to sea from the rock pools, looking confused. An empty sack hangs over his shoulder. We hear in a whisper, like the wind or tide, the voice of BUBBA.

BUBBA: Where? Where are you? There's cold underneath, it got real sharp fingers. It stick 'em right into me. Making me scared. No one sees me. Wheke he don't, he just stretch right through me. Got eight arms but he won't cuddle. Where are the faces? The mouths making kisses? Don't wanna stay here. All by myself. No one can see me.

      HOHEPA searches, as if for pāua.

TYLER enters the whare raranga and starts to weave a large tukutuku panel. His movements at this stage are small. A chair sits to one side of the panel, another nearby. He becomes dissatisfied with the work he is doing and walks around the panel several times.

TYLER: Shit! Fuck! (*He throws a chair on the floor in frustration.*) Aargh! (*He goes to the window and stares out at HOHEPA. To himself*) Koro Hohepa. They used to call you the quiet rangatira. Never made a fuss. Invisible and strong, like superglue. Now look at you down there amongst the weed and rocks, looking for pāua in a place where there ain't been nothing but sadness for years. But

you the man eh Koro? One day you're gonna snap right
out of it and give Te Kupenga a real shake up. Yeah. Fuck
yeah, you da man. (*Yells out to* HOHEPA) Any pāua today
Koro Hohepa?

HOHEPA (*looking around and finally up at* TYLER, *surprised*):
Eh boy?

TYLER: You get any pāua today?

HOHEPA (*confused*): What's that? What's that you say?

TYLER: Pāua. You get many today Koro?

HOHEPA: Did you say pāua?

TYLER: Yes. Pāua.

HOHEPA: Oh yes! Pāua. I got me plenty. Plenty pāua today.

HOHEPA/TYLER: Plenty pāua today boy.

TYLER: Same answer as always. We both know it's teka but
it's a fuckin' good answer anyway. (*Pause.*) I like you being
out there in the sea and I like Doris being up there in the
kitchen counting forks and plates. Hoping like hell there's
a few missing so she can kick someone's black arse. (*He
speaks like Doris, with his fist clenched above him.*) Who
the hell's been buggering with my forks? If they're not
back in their rightful place by tomorrow morning you
fullas better watch out. I'll be sending a forking war party
after your thieving nonos. (*Pause.*) The three of us, we
keep each other company in a no hassle kinda way. Me

down here spinning out with my tukutuku, Doris up there going crazy with counting, and you out there, pōrangi as, with your pretend pāua. (*He goes back to his weaving.*)

MATA *enters, followed by a nervous* RAMARI.

RAMARI: Kia ora, Tyler. Hard at work I see.

> TYLER *looks over at them.* MATA *stands behind* RAMARI, *squeezing her shoulders.*

MATA: This is Ramari, she's a whanaunga of ours. Came all the way from Christchurch to help with the preparations.

TYLER: Yeah?

RAMARI: Tēnā koe, Tyler.

> *For a moment,* TYLER *looks at them both suspiciously, then gives* RAMARI *a kiss and goes back to work.* MATA *clears his throat and gives* RAMARI *a nod. He walks around the room looking at this and that and generally being 'inconspicuous'.*

RAMARI: Did you realise we've got just two weeks to go before the opening of the new house? How time flies eh?

> TYLER *casts her a look then moves away from her and starts work on the other side of the panel.* MATA *clears his throat once more.*

Not ... not that we have anything to worry about. There are fifteen tukutuku panels finished already. Ngāti Tūora finished theirs last week. The South Island iwi have sent theirs through and the Hamioras ... the Hamioras have done three. Yours is the very last one. Exciting eh? I mean we're all just waiting.

MATA: Waiting with bated breath.

Pause.

RAMARI: I've heard you're a really good weaver. (*Pause.*) Would you mind if I took a closer look?

TYLER *shrugs.* RAMARI *goes and looks at the panel.*

It's lovely. (*Pause.*) It's lovely, but you've still got a fair way to go.

TYLER: It'll get there.

MATA *looks over towards the pair.*

RAMARI (*asserting herself*): It ... it looks like you could use some help.

TYLER (*rolling his eyes*): Here we go.

RAMARI (*swallowing*): A bit of company might be just what you need to speed things up.

TYLER: I don't want any company, okay?

MATA *walks towards them, hands behind his back.*

MATA (*menacingly*): Oh, I think you do. (*He smiles at* RAMARI.) And our Ramari here's not afraid of getting her hands dirty, are you e hine?

RAMARI: That's okay. If Tyler wants to work alone maybe he should.

MATA (*holding up a hand in protest*): No. It's already been decided. (*To* RAMARI) Don't worry. I'm sure that secretly he's very pleased you're here.

TYLER: Fucking ecstatic!

MATA (*rolls up his sleeves and rubs his hands together*): Well, come on then. No time like the present.

> TYLER *keeps working.*

MATA: Tyler?

> *There is a tense silence.* TYLER *stares at* RAMARI *for a moment.*

TYLER: Let's get started then shall we?

> RAMARI *is relieved. Seeing that things are underway,* MATA *once more strolls around the room, picking up this and that.*

TYLER (*to* RAMARI): I need to see you strip first.

RAMARI: What? What did you say?

TYLER: You heard. Strip. I need you to do that for me.

RAMARI (*open-mouthed, looking at* TYLER): That's not funny!

TYLER: Well it's not a joke.

MATA: What's going on over there?

RAMARI (*between her teeth to* TYLER): Pervert.

TYLER (*loudly*): The kiekie. Using a shearing comb, size and strip it.

MATA (*to* TYLER): Never mind all the hoo-ha, just let her weave the damn thing.

> TYLER *gets a chair and places it at the back of the panel.*

RAMARI: I thought I could start at the front.

TYLER: You're lucky I'm letting you work on the back. (*He unwraps a towel full of wet kiekie.*) See this? This is wet kiekie. This side of the kiekie is the puku.

RAMARI: I see, because it's fat like a tummy. Very clever.

TYLER: When I say puku up, thread it through the gap this way. (*He demonstrates.*)

MATA (*nearby, examining a piece of kiekie*): Good on you boy for doing this kinda stuff. (*Pause.*) Weaving. (*Pause.*)

Mahi raranga. Don't let anyone tell ya otherwise. Plenty of mana in doing this … this stuff, yes there is, it's not just for the women you know. (*Pause.*) Doesn't make a man go stupid at all.

TYLER (*holding in his anger*): Puku down means that way. To the urupā means through the gap to the left.

RAMARI: Sorry?

> MATA *wanders over to the window and looks out at* HOHEPA *in the sea.*

TYLER: In the direction of the urupā.

RAMARI: Urupā?

TYLER: Cemetery!

RAMARI: Urupā cemetery. Urupā cemetery.

TYLER: To the wharekai means …

RAMARI: Right. In the direction of the wharekai.

TYLER: To Koro Hohepa means diagonally down to the sea. (*The weaving begins.*) Puku up to the urupā.

RAMARI: Um, puku up … . (*She attempts to thread the kiekie through while she's talking.*) In fifty years time, my mokopuna could be sitting in the wharenui underneath this panel. They'll be admiring it and touching it and saying things like, 'Our kuia, Ramari, made this panel. See how stunning her stitches are? She was extremely talented.'

TYLER (*frustrated*): Put it here.

> *He pokes something through the gap so* RAMARI *can see it.*

No here. Here!

> *From his place by the sea,* HOHEPA *suddenly stands and, looking out into the distance, calls desperately.*

HOHEPA: Hoki mai!

> HOHEPA *then starts his search amidst the rocks again.* MATA *watches his father with distaste.* RAMARI *successfully threads the piece through and claps her hands.*

MATA (*still looking out to* HOHEPA): Stupid old bastard.

> TYLER *hears* MATA *and looks up.*

TYLER: What did you say?

> MATA *comes strutting over to the panel as if nothing has occurred.*

MATA: Ah yes. Purapurawhetū. Very significant. Very significant indeed. You know the story behind that one, boy?

> TYLER *ignores him, insulted at being asked such a question.*

RAMARI: Tell us, Uncle.

> *Out of* MATA's *view,* TYLER *mimics her words.*
> RAMARI *is amazed at his cheek.* MATA *clears his*
> *throat and walks around importantly.*

MATA: Stars in the night sky. Each one the spirit of someone
… someone … (*Clearing throat again*) … revered who has
passed away. They watch over us, so the legend goes.

RAMARI: That's so … um, tino ātaahua.

> TYLER *imitates her again and curtseys behind*
> MATA. RAMARI *reacts.*

MATA: Spies for God, you might say. You wouldn't want to
be getting up to any mischief while any of that lot were
peering down on you. Best kept for a cloudy night eh?

> *He pats* TYLER *hard on the back.*

Āe, āe, e tama.

> *He winks at* TYLER *and punches him 'playfully'.*
> RAMARI *laughs coyly.* MATA *comes close to her.*

Well just look at those stitches. You're a natural alright, e
hine. Wait till your mum and dad see this, eh?

RAMARI: They won't be coming to the opening. (*Pause.*)
You know mum.

MATA: Mmm. Well Christchurch is a long way from Te Kupenga you know. And I'm sure your cousins the Hamioras are taking care of you. You look like you could do with a bit of feeding up.

MATA *pinches* RAMARI. *She giggles.*

Well, I'll be off then. Looks like the the two of you'll polish this off in no time at all.

TYLER: Mata.

MATA: Āe?

TYLER: Nā Hohepa pea te taonga nā?[1]

TYLER *indicates a long piece of greenstone that* MATA *wears around his neck.*

MATA: What are you talking about?

TYLER: The taonga around your neck. It belongs to Koro Hohepa.

MATA: And he passed it on to me.

TYLER: He likes to keep it close to him.

MATA: I'd watch my words boy. Hohepa's my father.

RAMARI: Tyler feels Uncle Hohepa's his grandfather.

---

1 Doesn't that taonga belong to Hohepa?

TYLER: What?

RAMARI: You called him 'Koro'. (*Pause.*) When we were weaving. Koro means 'grandfather'. Everybody knows that.

TYLER: He's an elder! In Māori terms it's acceptable –

MATA (*ignoring* TYLER): Ah well, that's understandable. This boy here is missing a grandfather. Missing a whole family aren't you boy? Still, Doris did a good job bringing you up in the kāuta. Just look at that weaving. Bet you can cook a beaut steam pudding too, eh?

> *Shamed by* MATA's *words,* TYLER *stands and walks away to hide his face.* MATA *follows and puts an arm around him.*

Nothing to upset yourself about. At the end of the day we're all whānau. You can call the old fulla 'grandpa' anytime, just don't call me 'dad', eh? That might get people thinking.

> MATA *slaps* TYLER *on the back and laughs.*

Ka kite.

> MATA *exits, but not before planting a kiss on* RAMARI's *cheek.*

> *Pause.*

RAMARI: Do you want to talk about it?

TYLER: (*To himself*) Why? Why did he come back here now?

RAMARI: It's a good thing he did. All the old people have passed away, most of the young ones have moved on.

TYLER: And you think Mata's gonna solve our problems?

RAMARI: He's got the whakapapa, he's got the knowledge –

TYLER: Doris says the mana stayed with Hohepa.

RAMARI: It's been thirty years since the old house burnt down. We can't afford to wait another thirty for Uncle Hohepa to stop his pāua hallucination.

   Pause.

TYLER: This place needs some healing before we can do anything.

RAMARI: What do you mean?

TYLER (*facing* RAMARI): Why do you think everyone's left Te Kupenga?

RAMARI: There's been nothing to keep them here.

TYLER: They've left because of the sadness. Haven't you felt it?

RAMARI (*seriously*): Sadness? (*Pause.*) I ... I ... (*Her expression changes.*) This is another game, isn't it?

TYLER: No.

RAMARI: You're trying to make fun of me by coming on all spiritual, deep and very Māori. Well it won't work Tyler. (*She stands up.*) It's not like I wanted this job, not like I stuck my hand up and declared myself the in-charge-of-deadlines person, you know. They asked me. (*Pause.*) Mata asked me.

TYLER *stands and starts to walk away from her.*

RAMARI: I don't know why you and Doris bother helping at all!

TYLER *faces her.*

TYLER: These are our people, we work with them.

RAMARI: How noble.

TYLER: Yeah it is. And you know what else? You fullas can just sit here chewing your nails till I've finished this panel, and if I'm still weaving on the day the marae opens, tough. I'll be on permanent exhibition.

RAMARI: Well, let's see how the Aunties feel about that shall we?

TYLER (*mocking*): D-d-d-don't! You're making me scared.

RAMARI: Well you should be, 'cos they won't be just any old aunties. (*Pause.*) They'll be the Aunties from Motunui!

RAMARI *exits.*

TYLER (*calling after* RAMARI): Bring it on baby, bring it on! I don't need them or you or anyone else! You and your backwards crosses, your puku the wrong-way-ups, your poking-out knots and your split strips. You and your half-soaked, mis-sized, loosely-tied, unbleached bunches of kiekie! (*He walks to the window.*) Why can't they just leave us alone, Koro Hohepa?

TYLER *exits.*

> HOHEPA *stands, holding his sack, looking out to sea.*

HOHEPA: Such a confusing day, every memory lost. Even the green drop, the essence of you that once hung from my throat. Gone. (*He holds his hands to his throat.*) The clouds have covered the sea with their own image, and I can find nothing. Even Kawau emerges, dripping with an empty beak, shaking her head. The greyness leaves us all muddled. The rocks cut, coldness bites at my fingertips and leaves my body numb. Please. Tangaroa. Āwhina mai. (*He hugs himself, shivering, rocking.*) So cold, so cold and all alone.

Scene Two

Broken Promises

Early the next morning in the whare raranga. KUI enters. She is dressed in black, her hair and face partially covered with a veil. She walks slowly around the room, checking it out with the help of a gnarled piece of mānuka, which she uses as a walking stick. With her hand, she touches TYLER's panel and gasps. KUI slowly runs her hands over the stitches.

KUI: Purapurawhetū. Wairua shining in the night sky. (*She looks heavenward.*) How I long to see you up there dancing, e tama, dancing with your many relations. Maybe one day this soul might be lucky enough to join you. Auē, e tama, auē taukiri e.

TYLER *enters, muttering. He addresses his words to HOHEPA, who does not hear.*

TYLER: That Ramari, man she makes me sick with that born-again brown nosing of hers. And Uncle Mata. Uncle Mata! (*He imitates MATA.*) 'Weaving makes a man go stupid.' Still, coming from a 40 year-old make-believe kaumātua, I suppose anything makes sense. (*He takes some wet kiekie, which he begins to size.*) I can't believe none of his father's wisdom rubbed off on him. Koro Hohepa, you were an awesome tukutuku weaver. (*Pause.*) Wish you could help me now.

TYLER *goes to the window and yells to* HOHEPA.

Eh Koro Hohepa? You used to be a gun weaver in your day!

HOHEPA: What? What? Eh boy? Oh yes. Plenty pāua, plenty pāua today.

TYLER (*to himself*): Well, you might not be here physically, and mentally things might be slightly rusty, but spiritually? (*He walks over to the panel and ponders.*) Spiritually you're right behind me, eh Koro?

> KUI *slowly walks behind* TYLER *and puts her hand on his shoulder.* TYLER *is caught by surprise, turns, and leaps backward.*

TYLER: Aarh! Aarh! Who the fuck are you?

> KUI *sits down beside the panel, laughing.*

Shit! Help ... help! Hang on. Ramari? Is that you? Yeah, of course it is. Getting a bit of utu are we ? (*Pause.*) Okay joke's over. Funny funny funny. You got me. I was a stupid sucker and you got me. (*Pause.*) You can come out now. Ramari? (*Pause.*) Right, if you wanna play dirty.

> TYLER *goes to lift the veil.* KUI *raises her hand.*

Aargh!

KUI: The light, you silly boy, it hurts these tired old eyes.

TYLER: Shit! I mean ... fuck! Sorry. (*Pause.*) I thought you were someone else.

KUI: The doctor, he says it's the glaucoma, and those young ones, they say smoke some of our marijuana, it's good for the eyes. Ballyhoo. The whole damn lot of 'em speak a load of ballyhoo.

TYLER: Where ... um ... ko wai koe, e Kui?[2]

KUI: Āe. Yes, yes that'll do.

TYLER: Excuse me?

KUI: Kui. Call me Kui.

> TYLER *goes to kiss her.* KUI *turns her cheek, and* TYLER *kisses her veil.*

TYLER: I'm Tyler. Tyler Moananui.

KUI: Not Doris's son?

TYLER: Um. (*Pause.*) Yeah.

KUI: Good. You're strong. I can feel you're strong.

TYLER: Yeah? Thanks. Have you been here long?

KUI: Long enough to hear you speak blasphemously about half the folk in the pā.

TYLER: Are you here for the marae meeting? 'Cos they had that yesterday.

---

2 Who are you, Kui?

KUI: Marae meeting? Ah yes, everybody running round like beheaded chickens this way and that.

Pause.

TYLER: I get it, you're one of the Aunty brigade from Motunui. That was quick. Man, it is true what they say about you lot. Don't get me wrong, they say you're really beautiful and I s'pose shrinking heads was just a sign of the times, but, ah, listen, Aunty ... Kui, I hate to bum you out, but I am happiest working alone.

KUI (*standing up, looking at the panel*): Purapurawhetū. When someone special dies, their spirit joins the others in a wild tango across the night sky.

TYLER: Awesome.

KUI: Your work is good. (*Pause.*) Who taught you?

TYLER: Hohepa taught Doris when she was young, she taught me when I was a kid, me and the Hamioras. Not many of us left here, but I suppose you'd know that.

KUI: Mmmm, such a shame.

TYLER: I ... I really do like to weave alone.

KUI: Good, 'cos I ain't helping you. (*She holds her fingers up.*) Can't even peel a damn apple with these. It's the arthritis. I just come to sit and wait. (*She sits down with difficulty.*)

TYLER: Your being here won't make me work any faster.

KUI: Good.

TYLER: But I don't believe in deadlines.

KUI: Neither do I. You heard of Māori time? I'm ten times slower than that.

> TYLER *laughs to himself.*

RAMARI *enters.*

RAMARI: Tyler, I've been thinking. (*Pause.*) Maybe you and I should start again.

> *She sees* KUI, *is startled, and mouths to* TYLER.

Who is this?

TYLER (*loudly*): You mean you don't know?

RAMARI (*embarrassed*): We haven't been introduced.

TYLER: This is Kui.

> RAMARI *nervously straightens herself and approaches* KUI. *She takes a deep breath, shuts her eyes, extends her hand and attempts to hongi* KUI, *who extends neither hand nor nose.* RAMARI *is left feeling stupid.*

RAMARI: Ah … I … I … Tēnā koe, e Kui. Ko Ramari ahau.[3]

KUI: So? That's your bad luck.

RAMARI *backs away.* TYLER *laughs.*

TYLER: Kui has come to help me with the panel.

RAMARI: I didn't send for anyone.

TYLER: Must've been the others then. They mustn't trust you, Ramari.

RAMARI: Mata would've said something.

TYLER: But he didn't.

Pause.

RAMARI: Is there anything I can do to help?

No reply. TYLER *starts to weave.* RAMARI *stands awkwardly. She is hurt.*

RAMARI: Um. I … I should go then. Ka kite e Kui.

KUI: Not too soon I hope.

RAMARI *looks like she's going to burst into tears. She exits.*

KUI: Is she pretty?

---

3 Greetings, Kui. I am Ramari.

TYLER: Ramari? She'd look pretty good to a guy who'd been stuck in jail for fifty years.

> *They both laugh.* KUI *walks to the window and looks out at* HOHEPA. *She can see nothing.*

KUI: That ... that old fulla still out there in the water?

TYLER: Yeah, Hohepa's still there. He thinks he's finding pāua.

KUI: Pāua?

TYLER (*walks to the window and yells out to* HOHEPA): Any pāua today eh Hohepa?

HOHEPA (*surprised*): Eh? Pāua? Oh yes pāua. Plenty pāua. Plenty pāua today.

KUI: Auē Hohepa. That's not your voice, not your words.

TYLER: His words all right. Says the same ones every day.

> HOHEPA *stands up, rubbing his bent back. He slaps his forehead with frustration.*

HOHEPA: No good, it's no good. The sun spills his light across the water and I am left facing my own reflection. In it I find nothing but anguish. Auē Tama Nui te Rā. Aroha mai ki ahau. Tukua iho ōu ihi kaha kia mutu ai te mamae o tōku ngākau. Whakamahanatia tōku tinana. Kei te mākatikati ōku kamo. Whakamutua! Kia kitea ai te mea e kimihia nei. Homai te kaha, te māia hoki, kia taea ai e au.[4] (*Pause.*) We have all three cried in this sea.

TYLER: They say he's pōrangi. Looking for pāua in a place where there's been nothing for years.

> *Pause.*

KUI: Hohepa's not pōrangi, just starved.

TYLER: Yeah, for pāua fritters.

KUI (*staring out at* HOHEPA): Auē. He ain't looking for no pāua, that's for sure.

> TYLER *puts an arm around* KUI. *Focus on* HOHEPA. *He kneels, and covers himself with his arms. A red light covers him.*

HOHEPA: Kaua e tangi, kaua e tangi.[5] A much-loved prince, the hearts of the people were his. Passed from embrace to embrace. One cry would have us all singing promises to the tune of the wind. (*He sings an oriori.*)

---

4 Auē Tama Nui te Rā. Take pity on me. Let your warmth fill me, your rays take this pain from my heart. Take the salt sting from my eyes and let me see clearly what I search for. Give me the strength and the courage to complete what I need to do.

5 Don't cry, don't cry.

E tipu e rea
Whāia te mana o ōu tīpuna e
Kia puāwai ki te ao nei
Ka kitea ōu taonga nei ... [6]

>HOHEPA *is thrown to the ground. He remains there.*
>*We hear the voice of* BUBBA.

BUBBA: You left me. Left me. Sometimes I get mad 'bout that. I say words but Tangaroa suck 'em up with his big mouth an' you don't hear. I reach out, but no touching allowed. I want you to see, but they turned me invisible. Sometimes I get real mad 'bout that.

>HOHEPA *sits up.*

HOHEPA: Promises given and broken so carelessly. Sorry. I'm so sorry little one.

He exits.

6 Grow up and seek the mana of your ancestors
So that when you bloom
The world will see your treasures ...

Scene Three

The Quiet Young Chief

TYLER *is weaving Purapurawhetū. He steps side to side, from the back to the front, threading and wrapping kiekie. His movements are larger than before.* KUI *sits beside the panel. She tells* HOHEPA's *story.*

KUI: That poor old bugger used to be the world's most eligible bachelor.

TYLER: He's the true rangatira of this place.

KUI: He had land, all that land. Those hills behind the pā. (*She points with her stick.*)

TYLER: Yeah? (*Pause.*) Whose is it now?

KUI: Hohepa held this place together. He wasn't the only one, there were many of them, men and women. All working together. Māori are better at that than anyone else on the bloody planet. Even China. They had gardens here a mile long.

TYLER: (*He's heard this all before.*) With watermelon as big as houses and –

KUI: Hohepa was the quiet young chief, always working. Fixing this or that, and what a beautiful weaver. He designed all of the panels in the original whare.

TYLER: I know.

KUI (*shoots* TYLER *a 'stop interrupting me' look*): In those days there were no flash kitchens like the one parked up there now.

TYLER: Doris was still cooking in the old kāuta up until a few months ago.

KUI: He was a good poet too, just like that other fulla, Shakespeare. (*Dreamily*) Hohepa's words of love were like golden syrup dripping off a spoon …

TYLER: Hohepa eh? You sweet talking ho you.

KUI: Oh … and there were plenty young girls waiting under that spoon with their mouths wide open.

TYLER: And I hate to think what else. Please don't take me there, e Kui.

KUI (*reaches out with her stick and pokes* TYLER): Te Kupenga was full of people then, young people, old people and the babies. Everybody in those days was busy doing the Lord's work. There was a grocery store here and a post office there. Even had its own dance hall. (*She sighs.*) The Half-Moon Corral. The girls would line up for miles just to do the rumba on a Saturday night with Hohepa. He was ripe for the picking you see. (*Pause.*) He'd already had his heart bust once.

TYLER: Eh?

KUI: Got a girl in the family way. She was from Timaru. A Pākehā. She threw herself at him. The parents didn't want Hohepa for the son-in-law. Too black. She had the baby, a bastard boy, and left him with Hohepa and his whānau. That's where he stayed till he was twelve years old. His mother looked a tekoteko in the eye when she was carrying. She looked at this tekoteko so long and so hard the mauri of the thing jumped right out and flew down her throat into the unborn child. Matawera came out as greedy and ugly as an Australian cane toad. Had a selfish nose. He'd walk into a kitchen and suck all the good smells up with one snort. Leave nothing for anybody else. Then he'd help himself to the kai.

TYLER: Mata?

KUI: Āe. Matawera. He stole pork from pots and money from pockets. He was a greedy little tāhae. Does he ... does he come back to Te Kupenga often?

TYLER: No. This is the longest he's ever stayed.

KUI: Anyway, then along comes Aggie Rose and steals Hohepa's broken heart.

TYLER: Just a minute, we were talking about Mata.

KUI: Aggie Rose came down the island from a place called Tū Mai, was meant to be passing through on the bus. She got talking to one of those country cowboys, he reckoned he was going to a big hoolie that night in Te Kupenga. He asked Aggie to be his partner.

> KUI *continues the dialogue but removes her headscarf and, trailing it behind her, walks to the space representing the sea. She has transformed into the young AGGIE. TYLER watches from the whare raranga. AGGIE approaches HOHEPA, who is searching in the sea. The distorted music of the familiar Fifties tune 'Save the Last Dance for Me' plays in the background.*

AGGIE: So Aggie Rose gets off that bus twenty stops too early. Winds up at the Half-Moon Corral in Te Kupenga. By the time Hohepa latched his sleepy brown eyes on her she'd dumped the cowboy and was leaning up against a wall. One knee up.

> AGGIE *stands near HOHEPA, one knee up against a wall. She slowly pulls a cigarette from her cleavage and attaches a filter to it. She takes a long drag and shoots out the smoke in a hard circular stream. All the while her gaze is fixed on HOHEPA. She tosses her head back and laughs.*

AGGIE: A-ha-ha-ha!

> *Hearing her laughter,* HOHEPA, *confused, stumbles around in the sea area.*

HOHEPA: Aggie? Aggie? (*He stands, looking around for her. Finally he sees her.*) Aggie! Is that you Aggie Rose?

AGGIE: Ha!

AGGIE *walks away from him laughing, eyeing up imaginary men and appearing totally disinterested.*

HOHEPA: My Aggie, darling Aggie, please stay, don't go. (*She continues to walk.*) I'll find him. I promise.

AGGIE *turns. She appears sad for a moment. They hold each other's gaze. HOHEPA is young again. He stands completely upright. They are now at the Half-Moon Corral in Te Kupenga. The music becomes louder. Slicking his hair back, HOHEPA approaches AGGIE, smiling cheekily but often looking at his feet.*

HOHEPA: Please allow me to introduce myself, my name is Hohepa. Hohepa Te Miti. And I can't keep my eyes off you.

AGGIE (*taking a long drag and exhaling*): You from here?

HOHEPA: Yes, I am.

AGGIE: And you really think I'm something do you?

HOHEPA: Yes. Yes, I reckon I do. Like Kōpū, the morning star, your beauty has me spellbound. I … I think I would like to weave it into a blanket, so whenever I felt the sunset too diluted, or the sea too grey, I could wrap myself up and let the very richness of you sink into my pores.

AGGIE: Well. That's what happens when you're around too many people with the same smile. You long for a bit of pepper on your chops.

HOHEPA: Would you ... would you do me the honour?

> HOHEPA *bows and extends his arms.* AGGIE, *hands on hips, smirks, laughs loudly and gives* HOHEPA *the once over. The tune changes into a tango and they dance.* HOHEPA *spins* AGGIE *and she twists away from him, laughing hysterically.* HOHEPA *tries to embrace the 'nothingness' that a second ago was* AGGIE *in his arms.*

HOHEPA: Aggie! (*Once again he becomes the old* HOHEPA. *He kneels in despair, arms outstretched.*) Aggie Rose. Please come back. Forgive me.

MATA *enters the sea area where* HOHEPA *is. He rolls up his trousers so he can enter the water.* HOHEPA *clutches the pāua sack to his heart.*

HOHEPA (*quietly*): Please. Oh my Aggie, my beautiful Aggie. Gone. Gone. No. Please no.

> MATA *looms over* HOHEPA.

MATA: Aggie? She's long gone. Left you for another man. (*Pause.*) E Pā? He aha tōu mate? [7]

> HOHEPA *doesn't look up, but begins to frantically search among the rocks.*

HOHEPA (*raving to himself*): Broken hearts, broken promises. The ebb and flow of sadness. Pulsing, covering. Must find the core. Let peace rest in this place of anger

---

7 Dad? What's the matter with you?

and torment. Te Rā, Marama, Tangaroa and Tawhiri, I beg of you. Help me. (*Pause.*) Oh Aggie, please believe me. I will bury this pain in the place where demons lurk.

MATA: E Pā! Stop this crazy talk! Aggie was nothing but a whore. She took a match and burned this place to the ground. Then she left you. (*Pause.*) The past is gone. Leave the dead and join the living. (*Softly*) Titiro mai, e Pā. Ko Mata ahau.[8] (*Pause.*) I need you to see me.

HOHEPA (*looks to* MATA): You. You know where.

MATA: For Christ sakes. Stop this. I am your son!

HOHEPA (*confused*): My son?

MATA: Āe! Āe! Your son!

> HOHEPA *looks up. He sees the pounamu dangling from* MATA's *neck and reaches for it.*

HOHEPA: There!

MATA: So you remember this. The hei pounamu, Mirimiri.

HOHEPA (*still reaching*): No. No.

MATA: Passed down the generations from father to son, and with it comes all the mana of our great tīpuna, Awatea. You promised it to me, remember?

---

8 Look at me, Dad. I am Mata.

HOHEPA *tries once more to grasp the pounamu.*
MATA *pushes him away.*

MATA: E hika! I roto i tōu kaumātuatanga kua wareware
koe![9] What good is this to you now anyway?

HOHEPA *starts to search amongst the rocks.*

Your time as a leader has passed. Everybody's forgotten.
When you die, all you'll be remembered for is being a
pōrangi old man.

HOHEPA (*shakily*): Looking for pāua. Plenty pāua. (*He looks
towards the whare raranga.*) Plenty pāua today, eh boy?

MATA: People used to look up to you. The old people
thought that when they passed on, Te Kupenga would be
left in safe hands. What would they think now, eh? What
would they think of these 'safe' hands?

MATA *takes one of* HOHEPA's *hands.*

Used to be so much … softer didn't they? Now look at
them. Blue to the bone. Oh, and these chipped nails, and
these fingers, raw and bleeding. In need of a good manicure
I think. (*Laughs*) How could anyone be safe in these hands?
Only person that thinks you're special now is that boy in
there. Oh yes, the whāngai is proud of you. (*He moves
closer and whispers.*) I know you can hear me, e Pā.
So listen, you owe me that at least. I've brought Te
Kupenga back to life. I've saved the reputation of our
whānau, our iwi! Can you see the buildings, the whare,
the new kitchen –

---

9 In your old age you've forgotten.

> MATA *takes* HOHEPA's *head and tries to physically turn it.*

The phoenix has risen from the ashes. I did it all for you. I carry your load on my shoulders now. There's just one thing, one thing that I ask. (*Pause.*) The land. (*Pause.*) You can't use it now. It's right that it should come to me. (*Pause.*) It's going to waste. (*Pause.*) I want to use it for the benefit of our people. (*Pause.*) Make it easy on yourself. Give me the title to the land. (*He stands, frustrated.*) I don't know how it's going to look at the opening. All those important manuhiri, the politicians, the dignitaries. The Māori queen, Winston Peters. (*Pause.*) Tukuroirangi Morgan. What are they gonna think when they look out the window and see this crazy old koroua in the sea looking for pāua? (*He turns towards* HOHEPA.) We might have to put you away somewhere where you can't hurt yourself. Or others. (*Leaning in closely*) It might be time to let the sea rock your baby to sleep, eh?

> HOHEPA *jerks his head away. He starts fumbling, muttering to himself.*

You can hear me can't you? Well then, give me the title.

> HOHEPA *looks towards the whare raranga.*

HOHEPA: Boy! T … Ty … Tyler!

> HOHEPA *returns to his frantic searching, muttering to himself.* TYLER *goes to the window.*

TYLER: Koro! Koro Hohepa! Did you call me?

MATA: Call? 'Plenty pāua today' was all the old man said. E hika, what else can he say? Now, can't I spend some time with my father without you butting in? (*Pause.*) Eh boy?

> TYLER *doesn't budge.* MATA *and* TYLER *hold each other's gaze.*

I suggest you get back to your work.

> TYLER *slowly retreats.*

Act Two

Scene One

Oh When I Look At You, You Turn Your Face Away

The beach. Night. HOHEPA *has gone.* RAMARI *wanders alone. She trails a long, thin piece of driftwood behind her. She looks up at the sky, littered with stars.*

RAMARI: Tyler's tukutuku panel, Purapurawhetū. Painted across the sky. (*She kneels.*) Maybe you can tell me. Kei whea? Kei whea te aroha? Kei whea te manaaki? Kei whea te āwhina?[10] (*She extends her arms and yells.*) I just want of be part of all this. (*Pause.*) Can you see a place for me anywhere?

MATA *enters and stands watching.*

MATA: There's a place for you right here. (*He pats his heart.*) If I could, I'd pluck each one of those stars from the sky and hang them around your neck. I'd take the cloak from Papatūānuku and drape it around your shoulders. After that I'd steal the tiara from Princess Di – ah – Princess Anne, and declare you the queen of Te Kupenga!

RAMARI: I didn't see you there.

---

10 Where? Where is the love? Where is the hospitality? Where is the caring?

MATA ('serenades' RAMARI *using his best Howard Morrison voice*):

Titiro atu au
Ka huri kē koe
Kei roto i a koe
Pīrangi mai ana
Haere mai rā
Ki ahau nei rā
He aroha tino nui
Haere mai.

> *He attempts to waltz with* RAMARI. *She laughs uncomfortably and dances stiffly. He continues singing.*

Oh when I look at you
You turn your face away
But in your heart dear
You want me only
Welcome, oh welcome
To you my dear one
My one and only, oh come to me.

> *He finally releases* RAMARI. *She smiles awkwardly.*

Well, I'm glad to see that pretty smile. For a minute there I thought you were going to throw yourself into the arms of Tangaroa.

RAMARI: Oh no. Just feeling sorry for myself.

MATA: What in the world has a beautiful girl like you got to feel sorry about? Don't tell me that Tyler's been giving you a hard time. (*He takes on a boxing stance.*) Leave him to me, I'll sort him out.

RAMARI: It's not just him.

MATA: You've got to realise young Tyler's a whāngai. He's not from here. He might just be feeling a tiny bit intimidated by you. (*Pause.*) After all, I have just crowned you the new queen of Te Kupenga.

> *Pause.*

RAMARI: Where's he from?

MATA: It's not something we talk about. We like to treat Tyler as one of our own.

RAMARI: I won't say anything.

MATA: Alright, I'll tell you, but you mustn't repeat this. It'd hurt our Tyler very much.

> *He takes RAMARI's hand. They sit. He clears his throat.*

Doris was staying in Auckland, visiting a family member in the hospital there. Well, the whanaunga pulled through, so, on the last day of her trip, Doris decided to treat herself to a movie. On her way out of the theatre, she turned around to see this 3 year-old boy holding on to her coat-tails for dear life. She said he looked scared. Scared and hungry.

RAMARI: That's terrible.

MATA: The movie was ... let me see ... I've forgotten the name, but it starred Mary Tyler Moore.

RAMARI: You mean that's how he got the name Tyler? He was named after –

MATA (*laughs*): Could've been worse. She could've called him Mary! 'Tyler' was supposed to be for the time being, while Doris was waiting for somebody to claim him. Nobody ever did. Suited Doris fine, she didn't have any kids of her own. Hell, she'd never find a man willing to … ah … never mind.

RAMARI: That's so sad about Tyler.

MATA: Sad? The boy's been mollycoddled all his life, doesn't know what real work is. Twenty-one years on and he's still clinging to Doris's coat-tails. And Doris, she swears now that Tyler was born from her very own womb.

RAMARI: Well this is his place now, these are his people.

MATA: His people? Bah! Tyler's people are the nameless, faceless, invisible dwellers of the street and you remember that if he tries to mess you around.

RAMARI: It's not just Tyler. (*She turns away from* MATA.) It's funny, really. Mum said I wouldn't like Te Kupenga but it seems Te Kupenga doesn't like me.

MATA: You're just feeling a bit insecure.

RAMARI: Everybody treats me like a bad joke.

MATA: It's part of being a new face. Give things time.

RAMARI: Even you.

MATA: Eh?

> RAMARI *stands and fiddles uncomfortably.*

MATA: Come on, you've started something now. For the life of me I can't think what I could've done.

RAMARI: Well ...

MATA: Kōrero mai.

RAMARI: You ... you undermined my role as ... as in-charge-of-deadlines person.

MATA (*laughs*): In charge of what? (*Pause.*) Oh, oh that. Of course. You must believe me, e hine. I would never knowingly hurt you.

> *He gets down on his knees and takes her hand.*

I refuse to be hung without a trial. You must tell me of my crime.

RAMARI: You ... you called in a Motunui Aunty without telling me.

MATA: Motunui Aunty? (*He stands up and shivers.*) Hell no.

I get the shivers just thinking about those women.

RAMARI: I saw her. She was helping Tyler.

    Pause.

MATA: Eh? What did she look like?

RAMARI: I ... I couldn't tell.

MATA: Was she old, young, fat, skinny?

RAMARI: She was all covered up. Um. Old. Old I think.

MATA: What else?

    Pause.

RAMARI: She was mean.

MATA (*frustrated*): Mean? Mean? What about a name? What was her name?

RAMARI: I ... I can't remember.

MATA (*trying to be nice*): It's alright e hine, take your time. It'd just help if I knew how she was connected ... we don't want just anyone working on our taonga now, do we?

    MATA's *dialogue overlaps* RAMARI's. *He stops listening after* 'Kui'.

RAMARI: Kui! That's it! ... and it was like her and Tyler knew each other. They were playing games. I introduced myself. I said my name and she just said –

MATA: Kui, I can't think who that might be. I don't know any whanaunga by that name. Now who ...? Maybe Doris called someone ... in –

RAMARI (*finishing her spiel*): 'So?'

MATA: Eh?

RAMARI (*upset*): She said, 'So? That's your bad luck.'

MATA: Oh, oh, right. Well I can assure you Ramari, you're not out of a job. Leave it to me. I'll get to the bottom of this aunty business for you.

RAMARI: No, please, I don't want Tyler thinking I narked or anything.

MATA: Your name won't be mentioned. Who knows, this Kui might be good for young Tyler, she might get him moving on that panel. (*Pause.*) E hine, kaua koe e mahara.[11] I'd hate to see those pretty frowns turn into wrinkles.

> MATA *brushes her cheek with his hand.* RAMARI *stares disdainfully at* MATA. *He meets her gaze and quickly withdraws his hand.*

---

11 E hine, don't you worry.

MATA (*clearing his throat*): Now come on, I'll see you get back to the Hamiora's safely.

RAMARI: Um ... No it's alright. I'd like to stay here for a while. (*Pause.*) I'm fine really. (*She looks directly at* MATA.) I mean, when was the last time someone was murdered in Te Kupenga?

MATA (*choking*): Right. Right then. I'll be off. Don't stay out here too long eh?

RAMARI: I won't.

MATA *exits.*

> RAMARI *goes once more to the water's edge. She kneels and looks into the ocean. Blue and green light cover her. She is suddenly overwhelmed by a feeling of intense fear and grief.*

RAMARI: You. What do you want?

> There is the sound of a child crying. RAMARI is unable to move, unable to scream. It takes all her strength to crawl from that place of pain. Finally she is able to get to her feet and leave. She looks back. The area is still bathed in light, which fades. She runs. KUI emerges from the whare raranga, drawn to the presence of BUBBA. She looks out towards the sky and sea, and begins to sing the oriori 'E Tipu E Rea'.

KUI:

E tipu e rea
Whāia te mana o ōu tīpuna e ...

> HOHEPA *is also drawn outside. He cannot see* KUI, *but he hears the oriori. He joins in.*

KUI/HOHEPA:

Kia puāwai ki te ao nei
Ka kitea ōu taonga nei.

HOHEPA (*softly*): You've come back.

Scene Two

Velvet Curtains

Morning. KUI sits to one side of the panel. HOHEPA is out in the sea. It's rough and he finds it hard keeping his balance. TYLER enters.

TYLER: Ata mārie e Kui.

KUI: I dunno what's so damn peaceful about it. Listen to that wind, and that bloody sea. All fired up about something. And I suppose that old bugger's out there up to his neck in foam.

> *TYLER goes to the window. He yells to HOHEPA.*

TYLER: You okay Koro? I'll bring you down a nice hot cup of tea eh?

HOHEPA (*just about falling over*): There's plenty … there's plenty pāua today.

TYLER (*to himself*): Auē e Koro. I wish you'd let me help you.

KUI: You two are close.

TYLER: I don't even think he even knows who I am.

KUI: He knows who you are.

Pause.

TYLER: I swear I heard him call my name yesterday. But then I went to the window –

KUI: And what did you see?

TYLER: Uncle Mata. Standing in the sea with Hohepa. He told me I was hearing things.

KUI: Matawera. Hohepa must've needed your help. (*Pause.*) He can feel your strength even knee deep in the tide. (*She thumps her chest with her fist.*)

TYLER: Kei te pai koe e Kui?[12]

KUI: I'm alright. Just a dancing heart.

She pulls out a hip flask of gin and takes a swig. TYLER *watches.*

Stop staring and get back to work.

TYLER *begins to weave.*

KUI: Let me tell you about this Aggie Rose. She didn't get close to nobody. The tighter Hohepa held on to her the emptier he felt and the more he wanted. Like a bottle of good gin, it can make you cry but you still gotta finish the

12 Are you alright Kui?

bugger off. (*She takes a long swig from the flask.*) Aggie's family had no money and no land. All of that was sold to a Pākehā fulla for a few bob, some horses (*Takes off the veil and holds it up*) and a pair of velvet curtains. Pretty soon after, they packed up shop and squatted in the backyard of some cousins further south in Tū Mai. You know what happens to Māori when they got no land, no papa kāinga?

TYLER: Bums them right out.

KUI: Āe. (KUI *leaves the whare raranga, and transforms into the young AGGIE.*) They were a brow-beaten bunch. Aggie Rose never got so much as a cuddle, never a taste of breast milk. Grew up on a mixture of flour and water. So she developed these ways.

> *The 'memory' of young AGGIE walks in carrying the velvet curtains (veil). She holds them against herself and spins around. She picks up a tin mug and, with her pinkie out, swills back imaginary champagne.*

AGGIE: Ha! Darlings, how lovely it is to see you all here tonight. On behalf of James ... James Dean and myself, I would like to thank you for coming. (*She blows kisses.*) Love you. Love you. Love ya you pack of useless bastards! A-ha-ha-ha!

> HOHEPA *hears the laughter and looks toward her.*

HOHEPA: Aggie. You've come back.

AGGIE *stops and looks at him. She puts down the velvet and the tin mug.*

I'm so sorry.

AGGIE: Sorry? You don't know me enough to be sorry. (*She smiles slyly.*) Yet.

HOHEPA *is young again. He stands straight and tall. He approaches AGGIE holding his hand to his heart.*

HOHEPA: Everything I need to know is in here. Nothing you can say will ever change that.

AGGIE: Well then, let me tell you a bit about my life before I became your kept woman in a two shilling a night bed 'n breakfast.

HOHEPA (*puts his finger to his mouth*): Quiet Aggie. All that matters is how I feel about you.

AGGIE (*looks at HOHEPA and smirks*): Yeah? Well, I'm not as pure as you'd like to think.

HOHEPA: Stop it Aggie Rose.

AGGIE *puts her hands on her hips and licks her lips, then prances around the stage.*

AGGIE: I was just a girl. My family sold me for a few bob and a couple of sheep to a Dalmatian gumdigger. A Tararā. Every day he made me dig in the swamps for gum and every night I'd come home covered in mud. (*She spits.*)

HOHEPA: That's enough.

AGGIE (*smiling at* HOHEPA's *pain*): Ha! I've only just started. Every night I would have to lie there on a bed of spiky mānuka while the Tararā poked and prodded and grunted his way into me.

HOHEPA: I don't want to hear this.

AGGIE: He never washed. (*She holds her nose.*) Smelt like a long drop in the middle of summer. (*She runs her hands over her body. Her face is covered with disgust.*) His hands felt like the sole of a working man's boot. His touch as tough and gnarled as the roots of an old kauri. (*Pause.*) I wouldn't breathe until he had finished. That way I was able to set my spirit free from its body. If I was lucky I'd pass out.

HOHEPA: Oh Aggie. If I had known, I'd have stopped it.

AGGIE: He had a mean temper y'know.

HOHEPA: I would've just taken you away. Kept you safe.

AGGIE: Huh. Took myself away. Stole the bastard's money, and got as far away from my family and the gumdigger as I could.

> HOHEPA *kneels before her and takes her hand.*

HOHEPA: I'll never hurt or mistreat you. Stay here and you'll never feel that way again.

AGGIE: I don't need you.

HOHEPA: You have me under your spell. When the morning light spills across my pillow I see your face. And in the blackness of the night the peals of your laughter echo down the valleys and into my dreams. I need you Aggie. Will you be my wife?

AGGIE *stands above* HOHEPA, *hands on her hips.*

AGGIE: And what do I get?

HOHEPA: Pardon?

AGGIE: How do I know that after we marry you won't run off with another woman and leave me, and any babies we might have, with nothing?

HOHEPA: I love you. Trust me.

AGGIE: Ha! Where the hell does that get you at the end of the day? Cast out or up to your neck in stinkin' swamp bog, that's where. (*She spits.*) I want guarantees.

HOHEPA *holds* AGGIE *tightly around the waist.*

HOHEPA: Marry me and everything I have is yours.

AGGIE: In writing.

HOHEPA: Pardon?

AGGIE: I need it in writing.

She peels HOHEPA from her and walks away, still facing him.

I want the title to the land.

HOHEPA is unflinching, gentle.

HOHEPA: It's yours then. The land, my money, my heart. All yours. I trust you with them all.

AGGIE can barely believe he has said this. HOHEPA reaches for her. TYLER comes between them, breaking the moment.

TYLER (*yelling*): No Koro Hohepa!

AGGIE leaves. HOHEPA becomes old once more.

No Koro Hohepa! You fool! You ... you broken arse! She ripped you off badly, man. She ripped the whole of Te Kupenga off. Stole our rangatira and our land. And all because you were thinking with your dick!

HOHEPA looks up at TYLER.

HOHEPA: Eh? Eh my boy? What's that you say?

TYLER: I said that thieving bitch is gonna turn up here with a pack of mongrels and take over Te Kupenga and all because you let her!

HOHEPA (*yells back*): Plenty pāua today!

TYLER: Stuff the fuckin' pāua –

KUI (*angry*): Kāti! Kei te hē ōu kōrero![13]

TYLER: He was sucked in!

KUI: That's enough! You're too quick with your tongue! Hohepa is the rangatira of this place. He may have married Aggie but nothing changed. He was still there for his people. Never, you hear me, never be disrespectful to him again.

TYLER: I ... I just don't like the thought of him being taken for a ride, and I don't like the thought of this land going to someone, anyone, who just doesn't give a fuck.

KUI: He may have been blind in love, but he wasn't stupid.

TYLER: He trusted Aggie Rose. That's pretty stupid if you ask me.

KUI: Maybe he knew she'd do the right thing with the land.

TYLER (*turns and looks at* KUI): So where is she now?

KUI: Still walking this earth. (*Pause.*) Only just.

TYLER: Does she still have the title?

KUI: Maybe.

TYLER: What about Matawera?

---

13 Enough! You're wrong!

KUI: His mother should've thrown him away as soon as she saw his tekoteko face.

TYLER: Maybe Aggie passed the land on to him. He acts like it's his, and he's Hohepa's only son.

KUI: He wasn't Hohepa's only son.

TYLER: Eh?

KUI: He had another. (*She stands and walks away.*) That's enough kōrero for now. I need to rest.

KUI *exits.*

HOHEPA: Ka rere atu ōku whanaunga wairua, ka mahue ko koe, ko au. Tāua tahi e tū wehe ana i roto i te pōuritanga. Kīhai he oranga ngākau, he rangimārie. Ko ngā matihao o Tawhirimatea e haehae ana i tōku kiri. Engari, pai kē atu tēnā i te wairua mamae e pēhi nei i ahau.[14] Together not touching. Neither finding comfort, neither knowing peace.

---

14 As the spirits of my ancestors leave this place, I fear we are both to be left here. Together not touching. Neither finding comfort, neither knowing peace. The wind's claws tear my flesh. But the pain I can bear, it is nothing compared to the ache of the wairua that covers me.

Scene Three

Drowning

The same afternoon in the whare raranga. TYLER weaves as if his life depends on it. His movements are stylised, dance-like. Exhausted, he stops, goes to the window and stares at HOHEPA. RAMARI enters. Her spirits are obviously down.

RAMARI: Kia ora. It's me. (*Pause.*) Your most fabulous relation.

> TYLER *looks over towards her, then starts to weave again.*

RAMARI: I guess having Kui here has really helped. She must be an awesome weaver.

TYLER: She doesn't even have to use her hands.

RAMARI: But ... but that's not possible. (*Pause.*) Is it?

TYLER: She weaves stories.

RAMARI: Oh. What kind of stories?

TYLER: Old ones.

> *Pause.*

RAMARI: Where is she?

TYLER: Out in the back room, having a moe. (*Pause.*) She's crook.

RAMARI: Oh. I'm sorry. (*Pause.*) Tyler, there's something I have to tell you.

TYLER (*turns to her*): Let me guess. You're going to tell me that Kui's not one of the Motunui Aunties.

RAMARI: No, I just wanted to –

TYLER: Well you know what Ramari? I don't give a –

RAMARI: If you'd just listen –

TYLER: You and Mata make me sick. The pair of you've got everyone leaping around like blue-arsed flies trying to get this whare open and the whole thing's nothing but a joke.

    RAMARI *attempts to interject*. TYLER *cuts her off*.

Wake up cuz! All the karakia and ten-hour-long karanga aren't gonna solve anything. We aren't ready for this!

RAMARI (*well and truly fed up*): Maybe you aren't, Tyler, but everybody else here is!

TYLER: Kāhore koe i te mārama, Ramari![15]

RAMARI: What? What did you call me?

TYLER: Here we go.

---

15 You don't understand, Ramari!

RAMARI: Just shut up. I'm so tired of listening to your shit! I mean you're not ... you're not even from here! Mata told me, he told me all about you!

TYLER: Yeah? And what did he tell you?

RAMARI (*shaking*): How ... how Doris found you at the movies, how you held on to her coat, how you were scared, how nobody wanted you, how –

She looks over at TYLER. *He is suddenly calm.*

TYLER: How I was named after the great American tipuna. (*Pause.*) Mere Tyler Moa. (*He sarcastically sings, adapting the theme song to the* Mary Tyler Moore Show.)

I can turn the world on with my smile,
I can take a nothing day and suddenly make it all seem worthwhile ...

(*He launches into the chorus.*)

Love is all around why don't I take it?
I'm gonna make it after all, da da da da da da!
I'm gonna make it after all.

Yeah right.

Pause.

RAMARI: I'm sorry. I shouldn't have.

TYLER: Too late and you did.

RAMARI: But I didn't mean it. (*Pause.*) You're meant to be here Tyler. It doesn't matter that you're a whāngai. Not me though. (*Pause.*) Tyler, the reason I came to see you was to say goodbye.

TYLER: Eh?

RAMARI: I'm going back home.

TYLER: You didn't give it much of a chance.

> *Pause.*

RAMARI: Thought you'd be happy.

TYLER (*with difficulty*): Well ... I ... I don't always feel a part of this place either, but you don't see me packing my kete and running on back to the movie theatre.

RAMARI: Nobody wants you to. (*She walks away.*)

TYLER: Now hang on –

RAMARI: I should've listened to my parents and stayed put. (*Pause.*) We had this big fight.

TYLER: They didn't want you to come to Te Kupenga.

RAMARI: And if I'd waited for them to bring me it just wouldn't have happened.

TYLER: So, do they even know you're here?

RAMARI: They'll have worked it out by now. I wonder where they found the car.

TYLER: What?

RAMARI: It was a bloody stupid place to put a fence.

TYLER: You're a typical kick-ass Te Kupenga wahine alright.

RAMARI: You think?

TYLER: We're not so different. Doris and the rest of them, they treat me like whānau. But sometimes I think about it, the truth, and I freak right out.

RAMARI: You can remember?

TYLER: Mostly just how it felt. (*He turns.*) I ... I see the blue jeans leaving me and I'm alone, all alone. And I'm scared. Man I'm so scared. I run up the popcorn-covered purple carpet dodging shoes, dodging legs. I can't speak. I'm so full of air I'm gonna explode and if I let it out my lungs will fill up and ... and I'll drown.

RAMARI: Drown?

Pause.

TYLER: You don't need water to drown. You can drown in fear, takes something real big to save you.

RAMARI: What saved you?

TYLER: A furry pink coat that looked like a marshmallow.
I licked it and stuck on and it pulled me out of the fear.
Let me breathe.

RAMARI: Doris.

TYLER: She brought me a Fanta.

RAMARI: I've felt that too. Drowning. At the beach. But it's
not fear. At first it brushes the outside of your skin so
softly you think it's just the wind, then it sinks inside,
filling you with sadness and loneliness. (*Pause.*) I couldn't
breathe. The feeling was so intense it made a colour. There
was blue and green everywhere. So sad and so alone.

TYLER: What did you do?

RAMARI: I told it to go and think really hard about ... about
the people who love me. It weakened and left a small hole
in the colour. Then I could get out. (*Pause.*) What is it,
Tyler?

MATA *enters.*

MATA: Kia ora, kia ora.

TYLER *goes behind the panel.*

RAMARI: Oh, tēnā koe Uncle.

MATA: Ramari tells me you've been having a bit of help boy.

TYLER *doesn't reply. Loudly*

The kuia.

TYLER: Oh, her.

MATA: Where was she from?

TYLER: Auckland.

MATA *looks questioningly at* RAMARI.

RAMARI: She ... it ... it seems she was just passing through on her way ... south.

Pause.

MATA: And what did she want?

RAMARI: She wanted to –

MATA *turns sharply to* TYLER.

MATA: Tyler. What did she want?

TYLER: To have a nosey at the panels.

MATA: Come here when I'm speaking to you boy.

TYLER: Kei te mahi au.[16]

MATA: I said come here.

---

16 I am working.

TYLER *steps out from behind the panel and faces*
MATA. *He looks* MATA *directly in the eye. Pause.*

TYLER: Pīrangi te kuia ki te titiro ki te mahi tukutuku.[17]

MATA: Ramari was under the impression she'd been sent to
help.

RAMARI: I jumped to a conclusion because, because she
looked like what I imagined a Motunui Aunty might look
like –

MATA: In future, if we have manuhiri, you send them on to
me. It's not your place to look after them.

> MATA *moves over to* TYLER *and, leaning in, grabs*
> TYLER's *face. He speaks so* RAMARI *can't hear him.*

Don't fuck with me boy.

> *He pats* TYLER *on the back and moves away. He*
> *smiles at* RAMARI *and kisses her.*

Ka kite e hine. (*Laughs*) Keep an eye on our Mary, eh?

MATA *exits.*

TYLER (*gives* MATA *the finger*): Wanker.

RAMARI: Why did we have to lie like that?

TYLER: Kui doesn't need to meet him.

---

17   The kuia wanted to look at the tukutuku.

RAMARI: But why? Mata is the –

TYLER: What? The great brown arsehole of Te Kupenga that we all must kiss?

RAMARI: You really should give him some respect.

TYLER: Has he ever shown me respect? And what about you? Does he respect you?

RAMARI: Yes.

TYLER: Ramari, I think it's about time someone told you. It is not Māori custom to pinch arse, kiss and fondle each other twenty times a day.

RAMARI (*wiping the kiss from her cheek*): I ... I ...don't know what you mean.

TYLER: Well, I can't help you then. (*He sits down and begins to weave.*) Do you know what an ōhākī is?

RAMARI: No, but my guess is that it's rude.

TYLER: An ōhākī is like a legacy. Before someone croaks they pass on a really important piece of information to the living, something they need to get off their chest.

RAMARI: A confession?

TYLER: Or it might be unfinished work or a prophecy. (*Pause.*) I think that's why Kui is here.

RAMARI: Are you saying that she's dying?

TYLER: Yeah.

RAMARI: My god! What's wrong with her?

TYLER: That's not the point is it?

RAMARI: Well, I think the cause of someone's death is fairly important.

TYLER: The point is, Ramari, the point is, I think she has a story to tell before she dies.

RAMARI: Her ōhākī?

TYLER: It started out as a story about Hohepa, but it's turning into more than that.

RAMARI: Are you sure this is for real?

TYLER: You think I'm imagining it don't you?

RAMARI: Yes … no … I dunno. Well, I know how much you care about him.

TYLER: For a minute there I thought you might understand. I was even gonna let you stick around awhile, try and convince Kui that maybe you're not that stupid.

RAMARI *is on tenterhooks.*

But maybe we'd all be better off if you did leave town.

RAMARI: No! I mean, I don't want to now. Please Tyler please. I've never been to an ōhākī before.

TYLER: Well it's not something you buy a ticket to, is it?

RAMARI: You and Kui won't even know I'm here. Promise.

TYLER: You blew it big time, baby.

RAMARI: Please.

Pause.

TYLER: You promise not to say anything about this to Mata?

Pause.

RAMARI: You have my word.

TYLER: You better start making yourself useful, then.

RAMARI: You want me to help you weave?

TYLER: See that pile of kiekie over there? Sort through it. Put the white pieces in one pile and the mouldy pieces in the other.

RAMARI: But I was hoping –

TYLER *glares at* RAMARI. *She gets started on the mouldy kiekie.*

Act Three

Scene One

Whaikōrero

Later that afternoon on the beach. MATA enters. He picks up RAMARI's stick and tries a few taiaha moves. He rubs Mirimiri, the pounamu. HOHEPA (MATA's audience) searches desperately in the sea nearby, muttering to himself.

MATA: So you see, the woman will call the manuhiri on, and they will seat themselves along the paepae in order of importance. I will then speak. Firstly I will greet the manuhiri ... . (*He raises his stick in the air.*) E te pirimia, tēnā koe. Winitana, te tumuaki tuarua o te kāwanatanga, tēnā koe. Te Arikinui Te Atairangikaahu, nau mai haere mai![18] (*MATA is not an accomplished speaker. He spends much of his time clearing his throat, mumbling his way through things, and making dramatic gestures.*) And I want to say to you all, what an honour, a great privilege to have men and ... and women ... of such standing, such mana here in our humble village of Te Kupenga. See how the sky cries. (*Clears his throat*) A great sign, a very great sign indeed. (*To himself*) Then, of course, I will talk about how ... how things fell apart for a while, te mea te mea. (*Loudly*) But with the strength of my people behind me, I have managed to, ah, resurrect, yes, that's it, to resurrect (*Stands with arms outstretched*) the mana of Te Kupenga, and there it stands ... yes, there it stands, in its, in its ... entirety. Ko

---

18   Prime minister, greetings to you. Winston, the deputy prime minister, greetings to you. The Māori queen, Dame Te Atairangikaahu, welcome, come forth!

tāu rourou, ko tāku rourou, ka ora te iwi. With your food basket, and my food basket, we shall feed the people. And at the end of the day, that's what it's all about, isn't it? Togetherness. (*To himself*) After that my waiata. Āe, āe, I'll get everyone together for a singalong tonight. I must think about how I can subtlety ... subtly slip something in about my interest in the New Zealand First party. Maybe I should do it during the informal part of the evening, over kai maybe. Āe. That fulla Tau Henare's got a nice face. (*To* HOHEPA, *genuinely*) E Pā, what do you think? Not bad eh? I ... I admit the art of whaikōrero is something I never had the opportunity to learn fully. I ... I wasn't here with you long enough. But I do have your blood coursing through my veins as well as ... as hers. She had just remarried you know, when you sent me back. He ... he was an accountant. I ... I was an unwelcome surprise I think. I missed it here so much. Dad? Dad?

HOHEPA: Awatea. Awatea. Awatea was to be his name.

MATA: I ... I would've done anything to stay with you, e Pā.

HOHEPA: But Bubba he is still.

MATA: Jesus Christ! Nothing's changed has it? Look at you, a simple beaten old man, and you still haven't got any time for me. But still, all is not lost. The land remains. Have you been thinking about that?

He kneels over HOHEPA. HOHEPA *starts to panic.*

HOHEPA: No.

88

MATA: He aha?[19]

HOHEPA: Never.

MATA: Anō. Whakarongo mai![20]

HOHEPA: Never.

>MATA *grabs* HOHEPA *roughly around the collar.* HOHEPA *cries meekly.*

Plenty pāua today boy!

MATA: He can't hear you.

HOHEPA (*looks around frantically*): Aggie! Bubba! Bubba!

MATA: Bubba! You want Bubba? Maybe you should search properly. Let me help you.

>*He takes* HOHEPA's *head and dips it into the sea.*

See anything?

>*He lifts* HOHEPA's *head up.* HOHEPA *coughs and spits.*

You could make it so much easier on yourself.

---

19 What?
20 Again. Listen to me!

HOHEPA (*holds his hands up in protest*): Don't! Don't! He doesn't like the coolness, the deep silence of the sea. He needs the people. I have to find him. Please leave me. I haven't got what you ask.

MATA: What do you mean?

HOHEPA: She has it.

MATA: Who?

HOHEPA: Aggie. My dear Aggie, it's safe with her.

MATA: What? You gave that bitch the land? Who else knows this? Who has records?

HOHEPA: He wore a navy suit and a red tie, and she was there. My old friend. Doris.

MATA: But ... but what ... what about me? You stupid crazy old man! How could you?

HOHEPA: She's here.

MATA: She's in your head, that's where she is.

> HOHEPA *looks up towards the wharenui. He smiles.*

HOHEPA: I heard her singing.

MATA *looks up towards the wharenui. He exits, with a mission.*

Scene Two

Bubba

TYLER *is weaving Purapurawhetū. RAMARI sits on the floor, sorting through mouldy kiekie. HOHEPA sits on the seashore, head in hands.*

TYLER: That's the story so far.

RAMARI: Doesn't show Uncle Mata in too good a light. The mauri of a greedy tekoteko, that can't be true.

TYLER (*laughs evilly*): At night he unzips his skin and becomes the half-man, half-tekoteko monster known as Super Teko!

RAMARI (*laughing*): He means well. Anyway, I'm more worried about the way he treats you than anything.

TYLER: Save it babe, 'cos the word round the pā is that Super Teko's looking for a Mrs.

RAMARI: Ha. Ha.

> RAMARI *holds up a piece of kiekie in her hand, looks at her pile and sighs loudly. KUI enters, moving with difficulty.*

TYLER: E Kui. I pai tōu moe?[21]

---

21 Kui. Did you sleep well?

KUI: My ticker was kicking up bobsidie, but I got a couple of hours in.

> KUI *feels her way around the room with her stick. She hits RAMARI with it and gives her a good poke in the ribs. RAMARI winces.*

RAMARI: Ow.

> KUI *pokes her again.*

Ow.

KUI: This wasn't here this morning.

TYLER: Kui, um ... Ramari's here because she wants to ask you something.

RAMARI: Eh? (*She stands up, straightens herself, and takes a big breath.*) E Kui. I was wondering ... I was wondering –

KUI: Spit it out, girl, before you choke on it and die.

RAMARI: Tyler said it might be alright if I sit here and work with the pair of you today.

KUI: Work? Who said anything about work? I'm not here to bloody work. Done enough of that in my life.

RAMARI: Well, is it okay if I just stay while you –

TYLER: Ramari thought you were one of the Motunui Aunties, e Kui.

RAMARI: We both did.

TYLER: Hardly anybody here's ever seen the Motunui Aunties. There's just these rumours.

KUI: Six sisters. Must be well into their seventies by now. Descendants of the great ancestress Hineora. She was kai tangata you know.

RAMARI: What's kai tangata?

TYLER (*looking at* RAMARI): She ate human flesh! What about the head shrinking? Tell us about that.

KUI: It has been said that a few early colonists were shipped back to the Mother Country in shoeboxes after visiting the ladies of Motunui.

RAMARI: No wonder Mata's scared!

KUI (*sighs*): They're all vegetarian these days. (*Signalling* TYLER) Mata should be more scared of this boy here than the sisters from Motunui. (*She points her stick at* RAMARI.) You can stay, but I ain't got enough breath left in me to answer any stupid questions. Got that?

> RAMARI *nods.* KUI *attempts to walk over and take her place on the other side of* TYLER's *panel.*

RAMARI: Is it very hard for you to walk e Kui?

> TYLER *rolls his eyes.* RAMARI *goes to help her.* KUI
> *protests by hitting her with the stick, but* RAMARI
> *is persistent and* KUI *finally gives in. She takes her
> seat behind the panel, and* RAMARI *begins to rub*
> KUI's *shoulders.* KUI *whacks her hands.* RAMARI
> *backs off.*

KUI: No. Don't stop! You've got a good touch ... but a bit
further down, eh? That's better.

> KUI *takes a swig from her flask and removes the
> veil.* HOHEPA *leaves the sea and makes his way
> toward* KUI. *He is young.* RAMARI *steps back and*
> HOHEPA *rubs* KUI's *shoulders.* TYLER *leaves the
> panel. He and* RAMARI *watch the memory.*

KUI (*dreamlike*): Aggie and Hohepa got married under the
old karaka tree on the hill with Matawera kicking Aggie's
shins the whole time she made her vows. Hohepa taught
her how to weave the tukutuku. Together they wove
Purapurawhetū. It was the first panel made for the original
house. (*Pause.*) By that time Aggie had given birth to a
son. Yes, Aggie Rose was starting to feel pretty damn good
about life.

> KUI *has now transformed into the young* AGGIE.
> HOHEPA *takes his place on the other side of the
> panel and together they weave.*

AGGIE: I like it here Hohepa. I like the hills, the sea, the
people, but for the life of me I can't get the hang of this
bloody tukutuku business.

HOHEPA: Puku up to the urupā.

AGGIE: Puku this, puku that. I've had enough. I'm getting callouses on my backside and I'm seeing double. Why can't I just sew this thing up on the machine?

HOHEPA: We're nearly there. Now come on, puku up to the urupā!

AGGIE: Taihoa, taihoa! I want to see.

She ducks under the panel and sits on HOHEPA's *lap.*

I hope one day I'll get to join them.

HOHEPA: Who?

AGGIE: The stars, but maybe I'm too wild. What do ya reckon?

AGGIE gets up and looks out of the window. HOHEPA *follows her.*

HOHEPA: You'll take your place alongside Puanga, the beautiful rata flower. (*He points out a star.*) See her? She marks the rising of the first new moon.

He wraps his arms around AGGIE's waist.

AGGIE (*slapping HOHEPA's hands*): Don't go getting too carried away with yourself. I think our baby's hungry.

She breaks herself away and picks up the veil, which now represents the baby (AWATEA). HOHEPA leans over baby.

HOHEPA: Tēnā koe, bubba. My bubba.

He goes to AGGIE and takes baby from her.

Look at him Aggie. He's so handsome, and calm like the sea on a day with no breeze.

AGGIE hovers over the baby.

AGGIE (*tickling* BUBBA): Our bubba. Cheeky smiling bubba.

HOHEPA: With hair as black as coal and skin as shiny as a basted pie. He sparkles with all the mana of his tipuna, Awatea. There's no other name for him, Aggie.

AGGIE: Awatea? I don't know, Hohepa.

HOHEPA: After he's christened, I'll give him the taonga handed down to me all the way from Awatea himself. (*He takes the taonga from his neck.*)

AGGIE: It's too big a name for such a tiny thing. I want to wait, Hohepa. I had a sister named after a tipuna. She died just a week old. Bled from the stomach. All because the name was too heavy for her.

HOHEPA: Aggie!

AGGIE (*softly*): Keep the taonga safe for him.

She puts the taonga back around HOHEPA's *neck.*

We'll wait till he's old enough to carry the name. Till then, let's just go on calling him what we always have. Bubba. (*Pause.*) Hohepa there's something else I want to talk to you about. (*Pause.*) Matawera.

HOHEPA: What about him?

AGGIE: He worries me. The other day I saw him, he'd taken a stick from the fire. The end was glowing red. Then he tied your cattle dog to the tree and he –

HOHEPA: He's a child. You've got to understand, if he's angry it's because his mother left him so young. Be patient.

AGGIE: I've kept my bloody mouth shut about this for months because I knew it would hurt you, but enough's enough. I've seen plenty of cruelty in my life. Usually I can see where and why it's escaping, but with Matawera? His comes from a dark place.

HOHEPA: For God's sake, Aggie.

AGGIE: It's not just the dogs, the orange butterflies, the crabs, my beautiful dresses smeared in cow dung. I can take all that because he's your son and we're whānau now. (*Pause.*) It's Bubba. I worry about our Bubba.

HOHEPA: What are you saying? Mata loves Bubba very much!

AGGIE: Mata knew I was hapū before even I did. He used to elbow my puku on his way out the door to school. Give me a good hard shove.

HOHEPA: Sure he's a bit rough at times, but he's a boy –

AGGIE: He made sure Bubba knew who was boss before he was even born. I'm scared, Hohepa.

HOHEPA: I can't listen.

AGGIE: You have to!

HOHEPA: How can you talk like this! You're his mother now. He needs you.

> HOHEPA *leaves and walks toward the sea.* KUI *holds* BUBBA *close to her, singing the oriori softly.*

RAMARI (*watching her with concern*): Kui. Are you alright?

KUI (*looking down at the bundle in her arms*): We called him Bubba till he was nearly two years old. Bubba. It doesn't even give you a feeling when you hear it. One hot day, while Hohepa was out chasing cows and Aggie was busy sewing on her new shiny black Singer, Mata took Bubba down to the beach. (*She weaves Purapurawhetū.*) Stole his father's fishing boat and put wee Bubba inside. He rowed, he rowed as far as his puffy 12 year-old arms could take him. Then he stopped, put down the oars. (*She stops work.*) Did he look into your eyes then, Bubba? So trusting, so full of love. And you ... did you reach out to your big brother? Hold out your wee arms for a cuddle? (*She rises*

98

and looks, squinting out of the window to the sea.) Mata picked him up and threw him into the sea. For a while it seemed he floated, cradled in a bed of black kelp.

KUI *is* AGGIE ROSE *once more. She screams with grief, and runs towards the beach.* HOHEPA *yells out towards the sea.*

HOHEPA: Mata! Mata, what have you done?

AGGIE: Bubba! Bubba! I'm here, I'm here. Oh god, oh god. My baby, my sweet wee boy. All alone. Hohepa! He's all alone, so cold. My sweet child. We have to find him. Must, must find him. Where is he? Where is he?

HOHEPA *and* AGGIE *crouch bent over, grieving.*

HOHEPA: I'll find Bubba. I promise I won't stop searching till he's found. It'll be alright, Aggie, it'll be alright.

AGGIE: I saw it! I saw it, Hohepa! At ... at first a dog but no, there it was, the yellow jumpsuit I made for his birthday. Bubba? In the sea? What's he doing in the sea? Then the oar, like a spear striking. *(She calls desperately.)* Matawera! Mata! Don't! Please no! Striking and pushing, pushing down ... and the yellow, my Bubba, gone.

HOHEPA *holds her.*

AGGIE: Hohepa, he needed us, he needed us so much! I should never've let him out of my sight. Does it hurt to drown?

HOHEPA: Don't, don't do this! It's not your fault, it's nobody's fault.

AGGIE: I never even let you give him his name and I haven't even got a body to cry over.

HOHEPA: I'll find him. I promise. We'll find peace again, Aggie ... but please, don't tell the people it was Mata. He's just a boy ... he didn't mean to –

AGGIE (*furious*): What? Didn't mean to kill our baby? He is dead, Hohepa! Dead, and all you can talk about is saving the monster that killed him. I told you, I told you!

> AGGIE *leaves, and walks to the whare raranga.* HOHEPA *walks along the shoreline, head in hands, perplexed.* HOHEPA *cries to himself.*

> *Pause.*

RAMARI: It was Bubba I felt. His loneliness is the kind that spreads and swallows. It swallowed the fish and scared the people away.

KUI/AGGIE: Aggie Rose left then. But before she left she did one final thing. She took a match and set fire to the meeting house. (*As* AGGIE *she strikes a match.*) Hohepa. You tricked me. Made me believe you cared. The love and trust I let grow in Purapurawhetū is gone now, used up. (*Pause.*) There was only one person who knew Aggie lit the fire.

TYLER: Doris. She would've seen from the kāuta.

KUI: Hohepa kept his promise to Aggie. He's searched for Bubba every day of his life since the drowning. He lets Bubba's spirit cover him. He takes on Bubba's sadness every day to save the rest of the world from it.

RAMARI: What about Mata and Aggie?

KUI: Hohepa couldn't face the boy again. He was sent back to Timaru. Aggie jumped on a bus, and carried the pain of Bubba and Hohepa around in a suitcase. Everybody thought she'd taken the baby and left for good.

> *There is a lighting change and a breath of wind. From his place by the sea,* HOHEPA *leaps back, amazed. He has seen his baby.*

HOHEPA: My baby? What's that? What's that you said?

> HOHEPA *collapses as if struck. Lights/focus off* HOHEPA *and back to the whare raranga.*

MATA *enters.*

KUI: Ah, we have company. I wondered how long it'd be before you'd come.

MATA: Aggie Rose. Hika! Is that you? *Pause.* My dear, dear stepmother. It's been a long time.

KUI: Not long enough.

MATA *moves closer.*

MATA: The years have been hard on you.

KUI: But you haven't changed.

Pause.

MATA: What brings you back here Aggie? The marae opening?

KUI: No it's more important, far more important than that.

MATA: How interesting. What is it then? Oh I know. Dad. You've come back for the old man. How sweet, after all these years a candle still burns. But surely you've noticed? He's not quite as virile as he used to be.

KUI: I wouldn't take Hohepa from Te Kupenga.

MATA: Then what can it be? Let me think, let me think ... ah, I know. The land.

KUI: The land? I've no need for that.

RAMARI: Uncle Mata just go, get out.

MATA: Ramari. You sound scared. (*Pause.*) I hope Aggie's not been filling your head up with those stories of hers. She trapped my father with fancy stories.

He puts his arms around RAMARI.

Weaves a web does Aggie Rose. She pulls you in so slowly, so sweetly, then once she has you caught, she reveals herself to you. (*Whispers*) Don't listen to her lies.

> KUI *sees the taonga.*

KUI: Matawera! You're wearing the taonga! You think that by taking his life, taking ... taking his taonga, that you can claim his spirit, his mana? Where's your shame?

MATA: Jesus! Why don't you tell everyone what this grand charade is really about? You're here because you want to sell up, make a quick buck. I'll make it easy on you. I'll buy back the land. So take your money, your lies and get the hell out of Te Kupenga.

KUI (*unflinching*): I'm here to lay to rest the spirit of my dead boy. I'm here to make sure no whare is opened on this land before the cleansing is done. I'm here to see that you don't take Hohepa's place. The place that should have gone to your brother.

RAMARI: Tyler what do we do?

> TYLER *signals to* RAMARI *to wait. Things are still under control.*

MATA: Don't play games with me! (*He moves to* KUI.) Give me the land. The land belongs to me.

KUI: It's gone. Signed over to one of the only people left here with a head screwed on his shoulders. A boy. He's young, but mark my words, he's the one.

MATA: What?

KUI: Your father's felt it too.

MATA: Who the hell are you talking about?

KUI: Tyler. (*Pause.*) Tyler Moananui. The land is in his name.

>   MATA *lunges for her. She falls.*

MATA: Bitch!

>   TYLER *gives* MATA *a swift kick to the genitals.* MATA *screams in agony.*

You! You thieving little mongrel!

>   *He goes for* TYLER, *gets him on the ground. Starts to strangle him.*

RAMARI: Tyler!

MATA: You think you can mess with me eh? Eh boy?

>   *Stands up.* TYLER *holds his neck, gasping for air.* MATA *puts the boot in.*

How does that feel?

RAMARI: Stop it! Just stop it!

>   MATA *kicks* TYLER *again.*

MATA: Should've done this a long time ago.

RAMARI: Get away from him!

> RAMARI *grabs* KUI's *stick and strikes* MATA *in the back and then around the head.* MATA *turns and spits, smiling venomously, takes the stick, and pretends to strike at her. From behind them* HOHEPA *appears. He carries his sack, which is soaked and leaves a trail of water behind as he walks. All stare in disbelief.*

TYLER (*softly*): Koro.

> *The chant from* AWATEA *is heard softly in the background.*

Whakarongo ki te tangi hotuhotu mokemoke e
Ko wai tēnei wairua e rere nei?
Rere atu, rere mai e pōpōroa ana te reo
Te reo whakahua te ingoa i tuku iho mai ki te
    mokopuna nei e
Ko wai? Ko Awatea
Ko wai? Ko Awatea
Ko Awatea, whiti whiti te rā hei![22]

MATA: Old man? This is no place for you.

---

22 Listen to the one who cries to be heard
Whose spirit dwells here still?
Flowing here and there
Longing to hear a voice call out his name
(the name passed down to him)
Who is it? It is Awatea
Who is it? It is Awatea
It is Awatea. Let the sun shine!

RAMARI *takes the opportunity to leave.*

MATA *faces* HOHEPA *wielding the stick.* HOHEPA *uses the driftwood as a tokotoko, like he is on the paepae in the middle of a whaikōrero. He pays no attention to* MATA.

HOHEPA: Eyes downward cast body curled, and through the mist they came. The velvet cascaded from her waist like a waterfall.

> *He passes the fallen* AGGIE, *cleansing the space around her with a spray of sea water.*

So beautiful it hurt to remember. 'Help me, it's been too long,' she said. And the weaver breathed and his fingers flew, breaking the spell. I am with you.

> *He passes* TYLER *and does the same.*

I am with you.

> MATA *strikes at* HOHEPA. HOHEPA *defends and moves.*

MATA: You're crazy! Get the hell out!

> MATA *follows.*

HOHEPA: From the bottom of the sea his fear turned into hope. 'They are weaving my story. Daddy. Please listen, please listen. See me. Find me. Tell them who I am.'

> AWATEA's *chant becomes louder.*

MATA: I ... I'm warning you old man! Stop this!

HOHEPA: And Tama Nui te Rā roared, 'Hear them and my rays will give you the strength to stand like the tōtara.' Tangaroa smiled, licked my feet with a teal tongue and became clear. I saw a beautiful child. Tawhiri picked him up gently and placed him in my arms. He stands with us now.

MATA: You're mad! Mad! Don't make me do this –

He raises his stick as if to strike. HOHEPA *faces him.*

HOHEPA: And who is the one who carries so much fear and anger in his heart?

MATA: You better run, you pōrangi old bastard! Run back to the sea, the sea will hide you!

MATA *strikes at him.* HOHEPA *strikes with a spray of sea water, forcing* MATA *back.*

HOHEPA: The one I must forget, must forget ... the one who took our wee prince to the sea.

MATA: Enough! You hear me?

HOHEPA: Come with me Bubba, come with me, I am your brother.

MATA (*starting to break*): I have no brother! There is only me, only me!

HOHEPA: Love and trust, all he knew, before the coldness.

MATA: He had his share! There was nothing left for me! You cheated me then, and you cheat me now!

HOHEPA: Listen to him! Remember him!

MATA: I'm telling you. Stop it right now!

HOHEPA: Give him his name!

MATA: I said shut up. Shut up!

> MATA *goes for* HOHEPA. HOHEPA *raises his stick.*
> MATA *drops to his knees and covers his ears. The*
> *chant becomes louder.* HOHEPA *kneels in front of*
> *him.*

HOHEPA: Ko wai ia! Ko wai ia?[23]

MATA: No! I can't … I can't –

HOHEPA: Ko wai tōna ingoa? Ko wai? Ko wai?[24]

MATA: No, please no. (*Upset,* MATA *calls out to* AWATEA.) Awatea! (*Pause.*) Ko Awatea tōu ingoa![25]

> *The chanting fills the room and there is silence, and*
> *a great calmness.* MATA *falls into his fathers arms*
> *exhausted.* HOHEPA *holds him.*

HOHEPA: So hard to forgive when love runs deeper than oceans. None of us are blameless.

---

23 Who is he? Who is he?
24 What is his name? What? What?
25 Awatea is your name!

Scene Three

Purapurawhetū

Split Scene. Between:

(1) KUI and HOHEPA, at the beach. The stars are shining bright. HOHEPA is calm. He stands with KUI, looking out towards the sea.

(2) TYLER and RAMARI, in the whare raranga, weaving Purapurawhetū. RAMARI sits at the front of the panel. TYLER ties knots at the back. While the focus is on KUI and HOHEPA, TYLER and RAMARI weave.

HOHEPA: His pain's gone, Aggie.

> KUI *strokes* HOHEPA's *brow.*

KUI: And yours too.

HOHEPA: We did as you asked. We went out into the sea today. Matawera and I.

> KUI *turns away.* HOHEPA *draws her back in.*

We gave the taonga to him and named him Awatea.

KUI: Awatea. Our beautiful Awatea.

> RAMARI *is relishing sitting at the front of the panel.*
> *She prepares to thread a strip of kiekie through to*
> TYLER. *Having done so she slips under the panel.*

RAMARI: Coming through.

TYLER: What? You wanna weave both sides now?

RAMARI: Well, it is in the blood you know.

> RAMARI *holds her wrist up to* TYLER's. *Pause.*

TYLER: Come on, only two stitches left to go.

> RAMARI *goes to the front of the panel.*

TYLER: Do both of them back to front.

RAMARI: Get real. It wouldn't look right.

TYLER: How else will your scabby grandchildren know which stitches their Nana Ramari did when they lie under this in fifty years time?

> *Pause.*

RAMARI: Okay. Puku up to the urupā. What's taking you so long?

TYLER (*fiddling with the kiekie*): Taihoa. It's split. This is your fault. There!

RAMARI: At last. Right, puku up to the wharekai. Move it man! Geez! And puku diagonally downwards to (*Glances to the window*) ... to the sea.

HOHEPA: Why don't you stay?

KUI: Because I can't, that's why. But I have memories. Good ones now. Of you and Awatea. That's enough.

HOHEPA: I'm so sorry I never found him so you could hold him one more time. At least see his face.

KUI: Oh, I see it, every night I see it. I ain't got much time left you see. (*Pause.*) I need to believe in something after this life, that's why I had to get him up there. (*Pause.*) So we can be reunited.

HOHEPA: He aha tāu kōrero?[26]

KUI: Time to stop looking for pāua, Hohepa. (*She points skyward.*) There he is. Our Awatea. And hell, I don't mean to be whakahīhī, but I reckon he's the brightest one.

They link arms and watch the stars. KUI and HOHEPA watch. TYLER and RAMARI are still. We hear the voice of AWATEA.

---

26 What are you saying?

AWATEA:

The place where I dance is an over place.
An above place.
From here we can see everything.
We touch and circle and laugh.
Mostly we sparkle.
My name is Awatea.